Aliisa's Letter

Aliisa's Letter

LEGACY OF FAITH

A NOVEL

For Linda
Carol Van Du Woude
July 29, 2010
Finn GrandFest

CAROL VAN DER WOUDE

Pleasant Word
PW A Division of WinePress Group

Pleasant Word (a division of WinePress Publishing, PO Box 428, Enumclaw, WA 98022) functions only as book publisher. As such, the ultimate design, content, editorial accuracy, and views expressed or implied in this work are those of the author.

Unless otherwise noted, all Scriptures are taken from the *Holy Bible, New International Version®, NIV®*. Copyright © 1973, 1978, 1984 by Biblica, Inc.™ Used by permission of Zondervan. All rights reserved worldwide. WWW. ZONDERVAN.COM

Scripture references marked KJV are taken from the *King James Version* of the Bible.

Poetry quoted from *Finnish Folk Poetry Epic* is used by permission of the Finnish Literature Society.

Cover photo by J.W. Nara, circa 1913.

ISBN 13: 978-1-4141-1531-3
ISBN 10: 1-4141-1531-8
Library of Congress Catalog Card Number: 2009906740

This book is dedicated to
my great-grandmothers, Maria and Ida;
my grandmothers, Mary and Eriika;
and my mother, Amelia.

Author's Note

THE CHARACTERS, Mine Harbor, the hospitals, and clinic are all fictional. Aliisa's character is drawn from stories about my great-grandmother, my grandmother, and other women who emigrated from Finland in the late 1800s and early 1900s.

Calumet, Laurium, Hancock, and Houghton are real towns. Red Jacket existed in the early 1900s and is now part of Calumet. The Hanka Homestead is part of the Keweenaw National Historical Park. Captain Hoatson's mansion is now the Laurium Manor Inn. The Calumet Theater and the Michigan House still exist in Calumet and have been restored. The Lakeview Cemetery dates back to 1894. Finlandia University is in Hancock and was once called Suomi College.

Old newspapers and local history books illuminated the copper mining era. Excerpts from newspapers that are chronicled in *Calumet, Copper Country Metropolis* gave me a glimpse of the time period. Clarence Monette's books about the towns and Electric Park were very helpful. The *Finnish American Reporter* has helped me stay in touch with my Finnish heritage.

I have quoted several stanzas of poetry from *Finnish Folk Poetry Epic*. The poetry provides a window to the oral tradition of eastern

Finland. The Finnish Literature Society accumulated a vast collection of authentic folk poetry. Three scholars worked on editing and translating this volume of poetry into English: Matti Kuusi, Keith Bosley, and Michael Branch.

The completion of *Aliisa's Letter* was made possible by my family's support. My husband and son, Dan and Joel, provided computer assistance. My daughters, Sara and Julia, added their insights.

Glossary of Finnish Words

aapinen	book for teaching the alphabet and spelling
hauska tavata	I'm pleased to meet you
Heikkinpäivä	St. Henry's Day
hyvää ilta	good evening
hei sitten	bye then
juustoleipä	a round, flat loaf of baked cheese, also called Finnish squeaky cheese
karhu	bear
Kuparisaari	Copper Island, referring to the Keweenaw mining district
Kalevala	collection of Finnish folk poetry that was published in 1849
kiitos	thank-you
Naisten-Lehti	Lady's Journal, a publication for Finnish women
pannukakku	oven pancake
piikkisika	porcupine
pulla	a moist rich coffee bread
sisu	perseverance or guts
Suomi	Finland

Chapter 1

"LORI, I'M AT the funeral. Call you later." Karin snapped her cell phone shut. The lady sitting next to Karin glanced at her and frowned. Karin whispered, "Sorry." She turned off the phone and gingerly put it back into her purse.

The pastor finished his prayer and Karin shifted in her seat, feeling self-conscious. The church sanctuary was small and the thirty-five retirees in attendance had noted her presence. The organist played a classic hymn, *Beyond the Sunset*. Everyone seemed to be singing the words from memory while Karin sat in silence. Each word was lingered over as the congregation sang in a slow and reverent cadence. "O blissful morning, when with our Savior heav'n is begun . . ."

Karin had taken time off from her job in Chicago to fly to Florida. She had met with Pastor Paulson and his wife just prior to the funeral.

His wife greeted Karin with a hug.

"You are Marja's granddaughter. You have dark brown eyes just like her," Mrs. Paulson said. "I feel like I know you since we've prayed for you."

"Really?"

"Your grandmother talked about you. She was proud of you . . . she asked us to pray for you to be safe on that big university campus. Oh, she talked about you a lot . . . we knew when you graduated from nursing school. She asked us to pray about your first job."

Karin blushed. She had not given her grandmother much thought or attention. Occasionally she had sent a note in response to a card or gift.

"Well, we're glad you are here," Pastor Paulson said. "As you may know, all of your grandmother's funds were used for the nursing home costs, her funeral, and burial. The last bit of money will pay for the transport of her body to Calumet, Michigan."

"Why is she being buried in Michigan?"

"She grew up there, and the family plot is there. Most of us in the church are originally from Michigan," Pastor Paulson said.

Mrs. Paulson nodded. "We're all transplants. We grew up in northern Michigan and moved to Detroit to raise our families. Then came to Florida to enjoy the sunshine."

"So, Calumet is in northern Michigan?" Karin said as she tried to process the information.

Mrs. Paulson held out her left hand, her palm toward Karin, thumb pointing up. "This is the Upper Peninsula of Michigan, shaped like a rabbit," she said. "The Keweenaw Peninsula is the tip of the rabbit's ear. Calumet is in the Keweenaw Peninsula." She wiggled her thumb.

Karin tried to remember if anyone had ever said that Grandma Maki had grown up in the Keweenaw Peninsula. Grandma Maki was gone and Karin was beginning to have questions that she would never get a chance to ask.

Mrs. Paulson interrupted Karin's thoughts. "I understand that you live in Chicago. Do you live alone?"

"No, I have a roommate. Lori and I have practically grown up together."

"Is she a nurse also?"

"No, Lori is in marketing. That's part of the reason we went to Chicago—lots of good jobs in marketing."

"Your grandmother didn't have much to leave you, but she wanted to be sure that you received some family albums, letters, and her Bible," Pastor Paulson broke in as he checked his watch. He indicated a large box on the table. The box was tied with string and had Karin's name scrawled across the top.

"Thank-you for making sure that I got this. Grandma sent me cards and notes, but I didn't see her much. I lost touch with her."

After a moment of silence the pastor spoke. "Well, we need to head to the sanctuary. People are arriving."

Karin took a seat in the second pew. She stood out in this group of people like a slender birch in a grove of oak trees. Her dark brown hair was cut in a chin length bob. The Florida humidity brought out her natural curl. She was wearing a black silk blouse and a multicolored skirt. The cell phone called even more attention to her presence.

Pastor Paulson began his message: "Dear friends, we are gathered here to remember our sister. She was an encouragement to all of us. We all enjoyed the pasty dinners that she organized for our community. Best of all, she was a great prayer warrior. We will miss her, but we rejoice that she's with the Lord."

He spoke about the promises of God found in Scripture. He talked about Marja's faith and the comfort that she found in God's Word. Karin listened with curiosity as the pastor read from the Psalms.

We wait in hope for the Lord; he is our help and our shield.

In him our hearts rejoice, for we trust in his holy name.

May your unfailing love rest upon us, O Lord,

Even as we put our hope in you.

After the pastor finished his remarks, the congregation sang *When the Roll Is Called Up Yonder*. Marja's church friends talked in hushed voices as they filed past the open casket.

Karin followed and viewed the shell of her grandmother for the last time. As Karin stood there, fragments of memories flashed through her mind. The gray hair, now streaked with white, was styled in the familiar bun that Grandma had worn years ago. Karin recalled the comfort of Grandma's lap and the scent of cinnamon rolls. The eyes, once bright and engaging, were closed. Faded pictures of her mother and her grandmother mingled in her memory. It was so long ago. Karin was only four years old when her mother died.

The church members filed into a community room where a couple of ladies had fixed coffee and set out some sandwiches. Karin noticed a clock on the wall and realized that her taxi was arriving soon. She had just enough time to make it to her flight. She thanked the pastor and his wife for their kindness then walked outside the church to wait for the taxi.

Karin was relieved to check her suitcase at the airport. Her arms were sore from juggling the box, her purse, and the suitcase. When she found her seat on the plane, she sank back and closed her eyes. As she relaxed and reviewed the events of the day, she realized that she hadn't called her roommate back. She pulled out her cell phone and called Lori.

"Sorry I couldn't talk earlier. I was at the funeral and the pastor was praying."

"It's okay," Lori said.

"I'm on the plane and should arrive at O'Hare around eight o'clock tonight. I'll call you when we touch down."

"Okay. Maybe I'll feel better by then."

"What's wrong?"

"Lots of cramps. The pain pills should help."

Karin was concerned but remembered that Lori was pretty dramatic during her period. After take-off she reclined in her seat and tried to sleep.

14

Karin was awakened by the announcement directing passengers to bring their seats to the upright position and fasten their seatbelts. The woman next to Karin tapped her on the shoulder. "We're landing soon."

After the plane touched down, Karin pulled out her cell phone. It was 8:10 p.m. After an exhausting day, she looked forward to a ride home with her roommate.

Lori was breathing hard when she answered the phone.

"Hey, Lori! Did you just run up the stairs or something? You sound winded," Karin said.

"No . . . I don't feel good . . . I threw up . . ." Lori's words were fading away.

"Are you okay to come and get me?" Karin asked.

"I don't know . . . feeling a little dizzy."

"Do you think you can drive?"

"I . . . don't . . . know."

Lori was speaking with long pauses and seemed distant. Karin made up her mind to get a taxi. "Don't worry. I'll find a way home—see you soon."

"Yeah . . . okay . . ." The phone clattered. Did Lori drop it? Karin waited. After a moment there was a dial tone. Karin was alarmed and anxious to get home.

Passengers began filling the aisles. Karin put away her phone, and the woman next to her gathered her bags. As Karin waited to exit the plane she remembered that she was out of cash; she would have to find an ATM first.

Karin paid the taxi driver and, clutching her bags, hurried into the apartment building. She took the elevator to the third floor and dragged her stuff to the door of the apartment.

She searched through her purse for keys, pushing aside make-up, comb, wallet, and receipts. She breathed a sigh of relief when her fingers touched the rough edges of her keys. When she opened the door, she saw Lori stretched out on the couch. Her thick auburn hair was uncombed and matted. Lori opened her eyes as Karin came in.

"Sorry I couldn't come," she whispered. Her cheeks were flushed, and there was a bottle of pills on the end table next to her.

"What's wrong, Lori? How long have you been sick?"

"My stomach hurts bad," Lori said. She tried to sit up. Karin assisted her to a sitting position and noted her weakness.

"Did you have anything to eat recently?"

"Don't feel like eating . . . might throw up . . ."

"Do you have a fever? Drat, I don't think we have a thermometer," Karin said and instinctively felt for Lori's pulse. It was rapid and thready.

"Have you seen a doctor?"

"I got a prescription . . . yesterday," Lori said without further explanation.

Karin walked over to the table and picked up the pill container. The medication was labeled Tylenol with codeine.

"Why did the doctor prescribe these pills?"

"Bad cramps . . . I had such bad cramps," Lori said.

"Which doctor did you see?"

"Didn't see . . . called on the phone . . ."

"How long have you been sick?"

"Maybe . . . a couple days."

"A doctor just gave you this prescription over the phone?" Karin asked with astonishment. Lori's account didn't make sense to Karin. She was concerned about Lori and decided not to waste time asking more questions. "I'm going to take you to the emergency room at Northland."

Lori protested but Karin was firm. "We're going to the emergency room."

Karin walked Lori down to the apartment entrance. When they reached the steps, Lori sank down to a sitting position. " . . . need to rest . . ."

"Okay, wait here. I'll get my car," Karin said. She jogged to her car, slipped into the driver's seat, and put the key in the ignition with shaking fingers. She drove to the apartment entrance and jumped out of the car to assist Lori into the passenger seat.

Karin's mind was racing as she drove to the hospital. Her usually energetic roommate was listless, weak, and flushed. Her breathing was rapid, and she spoke in short sentences. Karin wondered, what kind of illness is this?

When they got to the hospital, Karin had to assist Lori to the emergency room entrance. Lori leaned heavily on Karin's arm. Fortunately, a hospital employee brought a wheelchair, and Lori sank into the seat. Karin went to park the car, and when she came back Lori had been taken into triage. Karin was asked to wait in the waiting room.

Karin glanced around the waiting room. She saw an old man with white hair sitting by himself and across from him, a couple with a toddler. She settled in a chair and wondered how long it would take. She noticed a clock—it was already 11:30 p.m. Karin hoped Lori would be treated quickly.

Karin had grabbed a sweater when she left the apartment but left it in the car. The waiting room was cool, and she shivered in her thin blouse. She got up and paced, then went to the car to get the sweater. She came back hugging it and approached the nurses' desk.

She was asked to wait a few minutes. When a half hour had passed, Lori's nurse appeared at the desk. "You can come and see her. We are going to be admitting her as soon as she is assigned a bed."

"Why is she being admitted?" Karin knew better than to ask this question. The HIPAA rules governed patient privacy. As a student nurse she had learned about the Health Insurance Portability and Accountability Act, which restricted the flow of information. A patient's health care was a private matter; only the patient could disclose information about herself.

"You can speak to Lori briefly. She is quite sick," the nurse said.

Karin wrinkled her nose as she passed a cubicle emitting a strong smell of urine. She entered the curtained room where Lori was resting on a stretcher and noted the intravenous fluids running. Lori was wearing an oxygen mask. "Hey honey, I hear that they are going to keep you overnight," Karin said as she reached for Lori's hand to give it a squeeze.

Lori nodded her head.

"Have they decided what you have?"

"Some . . . infection . . ."

"Is it pneumonia?" Karin asked.

Lori shook her head. "Could you call my mom?" she whispered.

"Sure," Karin replied. "Do you want me to call Mike?"

Lori shook her head. "No . . . we . . . broke . . . up." Her lips trembled and she struggled to control emotion. She turned her face away from Karin.

"Oh Lori, I'm sorry." Karin leaned down to hug Lori. Lori's shoulders were shaking and she sank back against the stretcher in exhaustion.

The nurse appeared in the doorway. "We're getting ready to move Lori. It's time for you to say goodnight."

"Hang in there, Lori. I'll call your mom, and I'll be back in the morning," Karin said as she left.

It was 1:30 a.m. when Karin stumbled into her apartment. She decided it was too late to call Mrs. Sander. She set the alarm for 7:00 a.m., planning to catch Lori's mom before she left for work. Too worn-out to unpack, she slipped into bed and fell asleep.

When the alarm rang Karin reached to shut it off and tried to remember what day it was. Was she going to work? And then she sat bolt upright. Lori! Lori was in the hospital.

After washing her face and brushing her teeth, she called Mrs. Sander. Lori's mom was startled to hear Karin's voice. "Karin. This is a surprise. How are you?"

"I'm fine. It's Lori. She asked me to call you. She was sick when I came home from Florida. I brought her to the emergency room at Northland Hospital, and she was admitted."

"What's wrong?" Mrs. Sander asked.

"She has an infection. She's very weak," Karin said.

"What kind of infection?"

"I don't know. I'm sure they're running lab tests."

"Oh, my poor baby. I should be there," Mrs. Sander said.

"I can give you the hospital phone number," Karin said. She gave her the number and reassured her that she was going back to the hospital.

Karin rummaged through her closet for a shirt and blue jeans and then headed to the bathroom for a quick shower. Her hair was still damp when she left for the hospital. At the information desk she was directed to room 259.

Lori was in a private room. She was pale and appeared to be sleeping. She still wore an oxygen mask and was hooked up to two intravenous pumps. Karin noticed that one of the bags of fluid was a powerful antibiotic. Karin stood quietly at the bedside, and Lori's eyes fluttered open. Karin reached for Lori's wrist and could barely feel a pulse. Karin pressed the nurse call button.

A voice responded on the intercom, "Can I help you?"

"Please send Lori's nurse in," Karin said.

"What do you need?" the voice asked.

"Send Lori's nurse," Karin repeated.

When a couple minutes went by with no response, Karin decided to intercede. She picked up the bedside phone and dialed 333. She spoke to the hospital operator. "Call a rapid response for room 259."

As the announcement was made through the overhead loudspeakers, Lori's nurse rushed in the room. "What's going on?"

"Her pulse is hardly palpable, and she's barely breathing," Karin said.

The nurse took in the scene, assessed vital signs, and began setting up the pulse oximeter. A minute later other nurses, a doctor, and a respiratory therapist were rushing into the room. The charge nurse spoke to Karin. "You'll have to wait in the family lounge."

"I'm a nurse," Karin said.

"But you are not on duty here. The lounge is down the hall on your left," the charge nurse replied.

Karin waited for a half hour, listening to pages for Dr. Norbert. She picked up a magazine several times but couldn't focus on any article. When she could wait no longer, she went out to the nurses' station. When she asked about Lori, she was referred to the charge nurse.

The charge nurse explained, "We're transferring her to ICU."

"What's wrong? What are you treating her for?" Karin managed to keep her voice steady but couldn't hold back tears.

The nurse sighed and shook her head. "She has a raging infection. The antibiotic hasn't worked the way we anticipated."

"Is that all you can tell me?" Karin asked.

"I'm sorry," the nurse said. She eyed Karin with compassion. "But perhaps you could help us. Do you know how long Lori was sick before coming to the hospital?"

"I was out of town for a few days and just got home last night. The week before she seemed to be okay, but we were working opposite hours and barely saw each other. I really don't know when she got sick."

The nurse said, "Look, why don't you get a cup of coffee and then go up to ICU? As soon as your friend is stabilized, they'll let you see her."

Karin walked through the cafeteria line, bypassing the doughnuts and muffins. She had no appetite. She bought a cup of coffee and added two creams and a packet of sugar. She sat down at a cafeteria table and then decided to take the coffee up to the ICU lounge.

Once there, she took a few sips of coffee. How much time had gone by? Karin was unable to gauge the passage of time. She walked up to the ICU nurses' station.

"I'm here to see Lori Sander," Karin said.

The nurse at the desk looked up but appeared frazzled. "It will be a little while. Respiratory therapy is adjusting the ventilator."

Karin blanched. "She stopped breathing?"

"Her lungs need a little help."

As Karin stood at the desk, an alarm rang in the fourth cubicle. Overhead the announcement went out, "Code blue, ICU . . . code blue, ICU."

The nurse at the desk grabbed the cart of emergency medicines and intravenous supplies. She forgot about Karin as she headed to the fourth cubicle. It was a beehive of activity. Karin stood frozen to the spot, eyes riveted to the activity. Were they working on Lori?

The minutes added up. Karin wondered if she should stay where she was or go to the lounge. A respiratory therapist came out of the cubicle. As he walked by, Karin sidled up to him.

"Excuse me. Was that patient a girl my age?"

He was startled by her question, and his eyes glanced over her appearance. "I guess, maybe."

"Is she okay?"

The therapist looked past Karin without seeing. He knew he wasn't supposed to give out information, but in the emotion of the moment said, "They just called it. She didn't make it."

"Oh my God!" Karin cried as she ran toward the cubicle. "Lori, Lori!" She burst into the cubicle and stopped in horror. The limp body of her roommate was on the bed. Papers and empty vials were strewn about the room. Gentle arms restrained Karin.

Karin was escorted to the lounge. The charge nurse offered to call the hospital chaplain. Karin shook her head. "I'll be okay."

"You can go in the room after we have cleaned everything up," the charge nurse said.

When Karin went in to stand by Lori's bed, the stillness of the room enclosed her. She gripped the side rail of the bed, her knuckles white. Lori was like family to her. A wave of coldness numbed her emotions. It was like the shock of jumping into a frigid lake and floundering in the water.

As Karin walked back to the nurses' station, she noticed a clock. It was 3:30 p.m. and she was late for her shift. She left the ICU, looking for a restroom. She washed her face, applied some make-up, and headed to the labor and delivery unit.

The charge nurse put down the phone when Karin entered her unit. "I was just about to call you," she said.

Karin explained what had happened. The charge nurse put her arm around Karin. "I'm sorry. You look like you need to sit down." She led Karin into the nurses' lounge where her colleagues were having a quick cup of coffee before beginning their rounds.

"It's not that busy tonight. I think we can manage without you. Why don't you catch your breath, and then you can go home."

A couple of Karin's coworkers approached, and when they heard what happened, they held her in a hug. Someone brought her a cup of soup, and she sipped the warm liquid. Then she gathered her things and walked slowly out to her car.

Karin returned to the apartment and was overcome by loneliness. As she looked around the apartment, she saw Lori's sweater hanging on a chair, Lori's shoes by the front door. Her throat tightened. Maybe she shouldn't have come home. She picked up Lori's shoes and sweater, put them in Lori's bedroom, and shut the door.

Mrs. Sander called. "What happened? When I called the hospital they said Lori was sleeping. And then they called to say that she had died. What happened?" Mrs. Sander's voice broke up. She was sobbing.

"I don't know," Karin said. She explained what she had witnessed and promised to be in touch.

When Karin went into the kitchen, she saw Lori's coffee mug on the table. Karin put it in the dishwasher and forgot why she had come into the kitchen. She wandered about the apartment for a bit and then turned on the TV and settled in a chair. The pictures on the TV screen were meaningless. She did not hear the words spoken, although the volume was turned up.

Chapter 2

BOTH KARIN AND Lori had grown up in Detroit. They attended the same high school. Both had gone to the University of Michigan. Lori had majored in marketing while Karin had pursued nursing. During college they had different roommates, but they decided to begin their careers together in Chicago. The economy in Michigan was slowing down, and the women were eager to move to a more promising setting. Chicago presented a diverse market for jobs as well as cultural attractions.

They had a shared history of losing one parent. Karin's mother had died in an auto accident when she was four years old. Lori's father had left, divorcing her mother, when she was three years old. Karin and Lori had a bond that had endured through adolescence into adulthood.

Karin took the train to Detroit for Lori's funeral. At the funeral home, she greeted Lori's mother. Mrs. Sander reached out with both arms and clung to Karin.

"I am so sorry," Karin said.

"Thank-you for everything you did," Mrs. Sander replied.

"Is Lori's father here?" Karin said.

"My ex?" Mrs. Sander shook her head. "I didn't expect him to show up." Karin thought that at a minimum, Lori's father could come to the funeral. At least Lori didn't have to know about his absence.

Karin was relieved to see her college friends. She had called Mary, a former roommate. Mary had passed the word and then traveled from northern Michigan to be there. She was in the midst of wedding plans but found a way to come. Karin wondered what her spiritual friend might say about this tragedy.

Karin respected Mary's unwavering faith in God and calm approach to life. But sometimes she thought Mary's outlook was too simplistic. As Karin approached her friends, Mary reached out to hug Karin.

"How are you?" Mary said.

"I don't know. This is kind of surreal."

"I'm sorry," Mary said.

In Karin's mind, Mary was a defender of God. She couldn't help posing the question to Mary, "Why did God let Lori die?"

Mary paused, considering her answer. Finally she asked, "Do you believe in God, Karin?"

"I don't know," Karin replied.

"I don't think God wanted Lori to die," Mary said.

"Then why didn't he stop it?"

"I believe God loves us and is grieved by Lori's death."

Karin shook her head in bewilderment. Where was God when Lori was in the hospital? Mary didn't get it. Karin changed the subject. "How are your wedding plans?"

"Things are coming together. You're still coming, aren't you?" Mary had asked Karin to be a bridesmaid. It was unspoken, but both knew that Karin and Lori had planned to travel together.

"I guess . . . Lori won't be coming with me." Karin's thoughts strayed to road trips that she had taken with Lori. The summer after graduation they had driven to New York State to visit one of Lori's roommates.

It was hot, and the car's air conditioning unit wasn't working. They rode with the windows down, singing along with their favorite CDs. Lori had a heavy foot and they were pulled over by a police car as they sped through a small town.

The officer had asked for Lori's license and glanced at it, verifying Lori's appearance with the picture.

Lori had smiled sweetly at the corpulent police officer. "I am sorry officer. I didn't realize I was over the speed limit. We're kind of anxious to find a restaurant for lunch."

The police officer warmed to the topic. "Ah, my favorite place is Betty's Diner. She has the best meatloaf on earth."

"Where is it?"

"Turn left at the next stop light, and it'll be half a mile down on the right. Now, drive carefully and watch your speed."

Lori nodded and said, "Thank-you, officer."

Karin giggled as they drove away. "How did you do that? He didn't give you a ticket. He hardly even looked at your license!"

Mary touched Karin's arm and Karin came back to the present. "Jenny might be able to travel with you. She couldn't come today but asked me to give you a big hug." Mary gave Karin another hug. "She doesn't want to travel alone. She could take a train to Chicago and then drive up with you."

Jenny was the other bridesmaid, also a friend from college. Mary, Jenny, Lori, and Karin had all lived in the same dorm the first year of college. Lori had moved out to an apartment with other business majors. Mary chose to share an apartment with the two nurses, Jenny and Karin.

"I'll have her call you," Mary said.

Karin spent the evening at her dad's home trying to sort out her emotions. It was the second funeral within a couple weeks. Her grandmother's funeral had been a warm tribute to a life of faith.

She told her dad about Grandma Maki's funeral. Then she asked the question that had nagged at her when she was in Florida. "Why didn't we visit her after mom died? I hardly knew her." Karin regretted that she had missed out on knowing her grandmother.

Mr. Lindale looked away. Karin thought he wasn't going to answer, but finally he said, "I never had a good relationship with the Makis. I wasn't Lutheran—I wasn't Finnish. After Anne died, I didn't see any reason to keep up."

"How did you and Mom get together if your families were so different?"

"I met Anne on a trip to Bob-Lo."

"Bob-Lo?"

"That's right, it's gone now—an amusement park on an island in the Detroit River. We had to take a ferry to get there. Someone invited Anne to go along with our group. We had a whole day together, riding the ferry, walking the grounds of the amusement park, picnicking. We just hit it off." He paused. "After that we went skating and to the movies. We talked about the books that Anne was reading. I showed her new places." His eyes misted as he recalled the early days of their relationship.

Karin encouraged him to go on, but he shook his head. Memories brought back pain that he had buried. He still felt guilt over the auto accident. It happened on New Year's Eve. He had enjoyed a couple of drinks that night. On the way home the roads were icy, and he lost control of the car. He blamed himself for her death, and he assumed that Anne's parents blamed him also. They never talked about the accident and Mr. Lindale avoided contact with the Makis.

Karin's thoughts returned to Lori. The feeling of peace after Marja Maki's funeral did not carry over to Lori's funeral. This one left her feeling raw and miserable. Her death wasn't right. Why couldn't the medical staff at Northland save Lori? What had happened?

"I don't know if I want to go back to Chicago," Karin said to her dad. Mr. Lindale gazed at his daughter with a worried frown. He had not known how to help her when her mother died, and he didn't know how to comfort her now.

Instead he pointed out simple facts. "You have a job and an apartment. Just find another nurse to share the apartment with you."

"I don't know if I want to work in a hospital anymore," Karin said.

"Don't give up. You can put this behind you," Mr. Lindale said. He knew it was important for her to get back to work.

Karin heard her father's words. He was telling her to push past her feelings. She had done it before. When her mother died, she had buried her feelings. She had locked compartments in her life.

She understood her dad's reasoning. She had gone to school and earned a nursing degree, so she needed to continue. She couldn't throw it all away because she was emotionally down. She had to earn a living. What else could she do?

Karin returned to Chicago despondent but resigned to continuing her job. Karin's manager assured her that the hospital had carefully inspected Lori's case. The hospital was required to file a report regarding Lori's death; it was a sentinel event. The nursing documentation, physician assessments, and treatment at the hospital were completely reviewed. The report stated that Lori's death was caused by septicemia, an infection that invaded her bloodstream. The treatment at the hospital was deemed thorough and appropriate.

When Jenny called, she was glad to have a distraction from the hospital. They made plans to travel to Mine Harbor for Mary's wedding. Karin looked up Mine Harbor on the map. It was in the Keweenaw Peninsula, halfway between Hancock and Calumet. It was in the vicinity of her grandmother's birthplace. Mary's wedding was going to take place in the copper country.

Chapter 3

The number of Finnish immigrants coming into the copper country is just as large as it ever was, and a constant stream has been pouring into this district all summer long, with no let up to it, being caused, in a great measure, by the treatment the Finns have been receiving at the hands of the Czar of Russia and his officials.
— *Copper Country Evening News*, September 8, 1899

KARIN'S GREAT-UNCLE HEARD news of the copper mines in America. Word was circulating about jobs in the United States. Matti wanted to leave Finland as the Russian Czar increased his control over the little state.

Life in Finland was difficult due to the scarcity of food. Matti and his family were farmers in northern Finland, struggling for survival. They relied on a cow for milk. They raised crops of potatoes, rutabagas, and rye that were supplemented by fishing and foraging. If the crops failed in the short growing season, as they had in previous years, they could lose the cow. In addition, Russia was leaning on Finland for military recruits.

When Matti went to the government office to get a passport, the clerk looked at his date of birth and shook his head. He told Matti, "Russia is demanding soldiers for their army. I can't give a passport to anyone who is eligible for the draft."

"I don't want to fight Russia's wars," Matti said.

The clerk shrugged. He had his orders.

Matti needed the passport—a document that listed date of birth, home district, civil status, occupation, and destination—to leave Finland. His cousin provided a plan for him. Otto had immigrated to America two years ago. He sent Matti his passport and detailed instructions for traveling to Hancock, Michigan. He explained that as long as Matti had a passport and could slip away to the Swedish border, the officials would not scrutinize the passport. He wrote, "Most of the border officials don't read Finnish and can't even spell our names. Swedish was the official language in Finland for so many years. When they see Finnish words, they just give the papers a brief look. They just want to see an official document."

Otto described a place called Kuparisaari. It was in the northern tip of Michigan and was the location of the Quincy Mining Company. The copper mining industry was booming.

With the passport and the promise of a mining job, Matti packed a knapsack with a change of clothes and some brown bread and set out for America. His destination was Hancock, Michigan. He told his family that he would write to them when he was settled.

When he arrived in Hancock, he found a thriving town with railroads bringing passengers from Detroit, Chicago, and Duluth. The town was built on a steep hillside, and the Quincy Mine Shaft crowned the top of the hill. The copper mining industry had developed Hancock into a port city with boats lined up at the docks along Portage Lake.

The town boasted a newly opened Finnish college, Suomi College. Associated with the college was a book concern, which printed books. Newspapers were flourishing as well as saloons, laundries, and barbershops. Most newcomers stayed in boarding houses.

A drawbridge over Portage Lake connected Hancock to Houghton, a gateway town on the opposite bank. Houghton had an established school, the Michigan College of Mines. The mineral wealth of the Keweenaw

Peninsula promoted study to identify mineral content in rock and ore. Engineers investigated the manner of locating, processing, and using natural resources.

Hancock was a bustling town, and Matti soon found work at the Quincy Mine. It was hard work: ten to twelve hour shifts down deep and dangerous mine shafts. The miners came from all different nationalities, and Matti discovered that it was difficult to communicate.

His cousin introduced him to a group of Finns that had decided to move to another mining town. Red Jacket was at the end of the railroad line that connected mining villages. Red Jacket sprang up with company houses built by the Calumet and Hecla Mining Company. Matti found a Finnish boarding house there.

Hancock was a thriving and growing town, but Red Jacket literally vibrated with activity. Bells and whistles marked the hours and signaled the end of a work shift at the mineshafts. Streetcars, horses, carriages, and carts rolled down the streets.

The business district was peppered with saloons and occasionally, a drunkard would sway from a doorway to the sidewalk. Sixty liquor distributors served Anheuser-Busch, Bosch, Pabst, and Schlitz beers. Each nationality congregated at a particular saloon. Matti visited the only Finnish saloon, but after a couple rowdy evenings at the bar, he chose to be temperate. Besides, he was saving money to bring his sister to America.

Matti saved a portion of each paycheck, and after two years, was able to send the money for Aliisa's transportation to America. She could buy a ticket that included passage from Finland to the United States and train connections to Michigan, through the Finnish Steamship Company.

Chapter 4

MARY'S WEDDING GAVE Karin a respite from work and her lonely apartment. She and Jenny left Chicago just before noon, too late to make it to Mine Harbor before dark. They brought some fruit and snacks to eat along the way. Their route would take them north through Wisconsin to Michigan's Upper Peninsula. The first part of the trip went quickly, because they had smooth-flowing traffic on the freeways.

Karin directed the conversation to their nursing jobs because it was a safe topic. Jenny was working on a large medical-surgical unit at a Detroit hospital. They compared charting systems and the computer programs used by their respective hospitals. But when Jenny asked about Karin's apartment and friends, the subject of Lori's death came up.

Karin struggled for words to describe how she had found Lori. As she explained the brief hospitalization, tears slipped from her eyes. She choked and caught her breath.

"For some reason she was taking Tylenol with codeine. I don't know if Lori told them about that prescription or why she was taking it . . . Maybe I should have mentioned it."

Jenny looked intently at Karin. "I'm sorry. I didn't mean to upset you."

"It's okay," Karin said and wiped the moisture from her cheek.

Jenny realized the topic distressed Karin, but she was puzzled by the unanswered questions. How could one of their group die suddenly?

"What was the cause of death?" Jenny asked.

"The final diagnosis was septicemia."

"That is unreal. It's so strange," Jenny said.

"I know."

The roads in the Upper Peninsula were one-lane highways. A light rain was falling, and Karin switched on the headlights. The women drove through long stretches of forest, occasionally passing a small town. Karin gripped the steering wheel tightly and shifted position. The drive was tiring, and the winding roads seemed to go on forever.

"How much farther is it?" groaned Karin.

"According to the map, we're not far from Chassell; then we come to Houghton, cross a bridge, and we're in Hancock. Mary's aunt and uncle live just outside Hancock. We are going to meet Mary there," Jenny said looking at a map.

"I'm really tired. Do you want to drive?" Karin asked.

"Nope, I'd rather navigate," Jenny said. "Maybe we should take a break. Besides, don't you need gas?" Jenny had just noticed the fuel indicator.

A few houses appeared amidst the fields and wooded landscape. Like buoys at sea, they indicated the approach of civilization. The two women were pleased to see a sign for a gas station and next to it an A&W restaurant. After filling the gas tank, Karin pulled into a spot next to the restaurant and got out of the car. The air was cool and she reached for her wool sweater in the back seat. Jenny zipped up her light jacket. Her red hair was gathered in a loose ponytail, and locks fell forward along her neck.

The fast food restaurant was not fast. They waited twenty minutes for their food. When they finally sat down to eat, Jenny remarked, "So you were coming home from Florida when Lori was sick. Were you at the beach?"

"No, I went to my grandmother's funeral."

"I'm sorry. That's rough—a lot to cope with," Jenny said.

"I hardly knew my grandmother. But I found out a bunch of things at the funeral. She grew up near Mine Harbor. Isn't that wild?'

"How come you didn't know your grandmother?"

"After my mom died we did things with my dad's side of the family and lost contact with her side of the family."

The conversation turned to the wedding and gifts they had chosen for Mary. Over an hour had passed when the girls returned to their car. When Karin put the key in the ignition and turned it, the engine turned over but did not catch. As she continued, the engine groaned but didn't start. "Something's wrong . . ."

"Let's see if the radio works," Jenny said as she clicked it. Nothing. "Try the headlights."

"They're on," Karin said as she went to pull the knob for the headlights. "Oh my gosh . . . I turned the lights on when it was raining and forgot that they were on. The battery must be dead."

"My car sets off an alarm if I turn off the engine while the lights are still on," Jenny said.

"Well, unfortunately this car doesn't have that feature," Karin said irritably.

The women decided to walk over to the gas station to get help. At the station, the clerk explained that the station's truck was out and he was unable to leave the cash register. The clerk called out to a man who was just leaving the gas station. "Bernie, do you have jumper cables? These women have a dead battery."

The man turned and nodded. His dirty jacket and the gristle on his face did little to recommend his service. But Karin and Jenny needed help.

"Could you help us?" Karin asked.

"Where's your car?"

Karin pointed to her red Ford Topaz.

He strode off and drove an old pick-up truck over, pulling up so that the hood of his truck was next to Karin's. Karin got in her car and released the hood.

"Stay in your car." Bernie bent over the engine and hooked up the jumper cables. As he walked back to his truck, he shouted, "When I signal with my arm, start your car."

"What did he say?" Karin asked Jenny.

"I didn't hear what he said."

Karin and Jenny waited while Bernie revved his engine. After a few minutes, he opened his window and waved. Karin waved back. Bernie shouted to Karin but of course she couldn't hear over the noise of the engine. Bernie jumped down from his truck and walked over to Karin's window.

"For crying out loud, start your engine."

Karin turned the key. The engine turned over a few times, caught, and began to run roughly as she gave it more gas.

Bernie said, "I'm going to remove the cables. Keep the motor running for a few minutes before you go." He removed the cables and let the hood of the car come down.

For an instant, Karin wondered if the hood was securely down but the engine sputtered and she focused her attention on keeping the engine going. Ten minutes later, Karin and Jenny were back on the highway. As they picked up speed, there was a loud thud, and Karin cried out, "I can't see!"

"It's the hood! Slow down. The road is beginning to curve." Jenny was opening her window, craning her neck to see on her side of the car. The hood of the car had flipped up obscuring most of the windshield. Karin's only field of vision was a small opening between the extended hood and the engine. Karin took her foot off the gas and slid down in her seat, straining to see through the narrow space of windshield. She saw that the road was curving to the left and began braking and turning the wheel, but not soon enough. The front wheels went off the side of the road and skidded in the gravel. The car stopped just before a shallow ditch.

"That was close!" Karin was still clenching the steering wheel. The motor was still running.

"I'll go out and close the hood," Jenny offered. She strained but did not get a lot of leverage in pushing down the hood the first time. Standing on her tiptoes and grasping the edge of the hood firmly she slammed it down again.

Jenny got back in the car. Karin checked her rearview mirrors and pulled back onto the highway. She was just picking up speed when the hood flew up again. Crouching down in her seat, she pulled the car over to the side of the road once more.

"What are we going to do?" Karin said. "We can't drive with the car like this." The daylight was fading, and the highway had few cars. It was a lonely road. She put the emergency flashers on.

Jenny pulled out her cell phone. "Do you have road service on your car insurance? I can call directory assistance to get us help." Jenny opened her phone and waited for the screen to indicate service. The screen read, "Searching." She waited but did not get a signal, not even roaming.

"I guess a cell phone isn't going to help us here." Jenny closed her cell phone.

Karin was about to turn the engine off when Jenny grabbed her hand. "Don't turn the engine off. We need to keep the battery charged."

Neither girl noticed when a rusty blue car pulled up behind them. The driver got out and looked around. There was no traffic now. He strolled over to the driver's side and tapped on the window.

Karin started and let out a little scream. A broad shouldered man, with light brown hair falling across his brow, was standing next to the window. He motioned for Karin to roll down her window. Karin cautiously opened the window an inch so that she could hear him.

"Looks like you have car trouble—can I help?" he said.

"We can't get the hood of the car to stay down," Karin replied.

The young man walked over to the front of the car and pushed on the hood, looked inside at the latch, and tried once more. He came back to the window. "Looks like the latch to your hood is bent. I might be able to tie it shut, but you'll have to bring it to a garage for repair."

He went back to his car, opened the trunk, and rummaged around. Jenny remarked, "I hope he's better help than old Bernie."

"Well, we don't have a choice," Karin said as she massaged the sore muscles in her neck.

The young man came back with a piece of heavy green twine. He methodically wrapped and tied the hood to the latch. When he finished he came back to the window and said, "This should hold, but take your car in as soon as possible." He paused and gave the girls a puzzled look. "Where are you from?"

Karin flashed a smile. "I'm from Chicago."

"What about your friend?"

"From Detroit. We're on our way to Hancock."

"I could follow you with my car until you get to Hancock," the young man suggested.

Karin was about to accept his offer, but Jenny spoke first. "Thanks but we'll be fine. I have a cell phone—we've got to get going." She waved him off.

"I wish you hadn't been so quick to turn down his offer," Karin said. "Your cell phone isn't going to help us."

"Oh, we'll make it okay," Jenny said.

"I hope so. We are in the middle of nowhere." Karin checked the rearview mirror and pulled out on the highway.

It was after nine o'clock when Jenny and Karin reached the outskirts of a large town. Jenny gasped. "Look at the lights and these mansions! After miles of forest, fields, farmhouses, and a few towns—this is amazing!" Two and three-story houses lined the road. Some had wide porches circling the front. Lights twinkled from the interior of these grand homes.

"Mary said that there is a university in Houghton and another one in Hancock. It is amazing to see this place emerge after miles of nothing," Karin said with wonder. "I'll need you to direct me now."

Jenny pulled out the directions that Mary had e-mailed. She directed Karin through Houghton and across the bridge to Hancock. The port that had once flourished with the business of copper was quiet.

They passed streets lined with closely spaced two-story houses that had been built by the mining company to house immigrant workers. The houses were on the steep side of a hill that overlooked the canal between Portage Lake and Lake Superior.

They were entering the Keweenaw Peninsula, which consisted of forests, scattered mining towns, and small Finnish farms. They drove to the outskirts of town and turned onto a recently paved road. Mary's aunt and uncle lived on the farm that had been in Mr. Aaltio's family for several generations. They found the gravel lane leading to a two-story green frame house.

Mary was waiting expectantly for their arrival and opened the door as they approached the house. She gave Karin and Jenny big hugs. "They're here," she called out to her aunt and uncle. Rita and John Aaltio came to greet them with the same welcome they gave family members.

"You must be exhausted from your drive. How about some tea? Are you hungry?" Rita inquired.

"We are sooo glad to be here," Jenny said, and Karin nodded.

The travelers told of their mishaps on the road while sipping hot tea. John said that he would take a look at the car and see that it was taken to a local garage. Then the conversation shifted to plans for the wedding on Saturday.

"My cousin Abigail is my maid of honor. She would be here too, except that she is tending to a woman in labor. Did I tell you that she's a midwife?" Mary said. "It's great that you could come a day early to help me finish up decorations and programs."

Mary could have bubbled on and on with plans, but noticing her friends' fatigue, she suggested that they all get to bed and meet for breakfast at her parents' home in Mine Harbor.

Rita showed the girls the second-floor guest bedroom with twin beds. Karin and Jenny hung up their bridesmaid dresses and rummaged through their suitcases for pajamas. It didn't take them long to get ready for bed, and Jenny was asleep as soon as her head hit the pillow. Karin tossed and turned for a while, her neck and shoulders stiff and aching. She finally fell into an exhausted sleep.

The girls woke to a sparkling morning. The sky was clear, and the sun reflected off the bright orange, red, yellow, and bronze colors that dappled the trees. Mary's cousin Abigail had come home in the wee hours of the night, but she was up when Karin and Jenny came downstairs. "I'm Abigail," she said, extending her hand. Karin and Jenny introduced themselves and noticed the firm grip of her hand. Abigail's hair was neatly woven in a French braid and she displayed a quiet confidence in her bearing. "Glad you're here to help Mary. We can ride over to Mary's home in my car."

The drive to Mine Harbor took just fifteen minutes. Mine Harbor was one of the little mining towns trying to make a comeback. A couple of buildings were in the process of rehabilitation. A general store and a gas station were among the few older establishments left. A small community hospital served retirees and a growing community of artists, entrepreneurs, and young people who were attracted to the rugged beauty and outdoor sports. The area was riddled with trails for snowmobiles in the winter and all-terrain vehicles in the summer.

Mary's mother, Helen Keskitalo, had fixed *pannukakku* and bacon for breakfast. Orange juice was on the table and coffee was brewing. The kitchen had an enticing aroma.

Abigail's eyes lit up when she saw a bowl of dark red jam on the table. "Aunt Helen's thimbleberry jam!"

"What is thimbleberry jam?" Jenny asked. "I've never heard of it before."

"Oh, you have to try it. It's like raspberry jam but richer. Aunt Helen makes the jam every August. She manages to take us on a trek through the woods and across gullies to pick the berries," Abigail said.

"We wear long pants and sturdy shoes so we can keep our footing. The berries are bright red—easy to see but not so easy to reach," Mary said.

Abigail turned to her aunt and smiled. "It's an adventure I have come to appreciate!" She slathered a wedge of pannukakku with the thimbleberry jam and passed it around the table.

The girls lingered over the pancake, enjoying a leisurely breakfast. Mrs. Keskitalo reluctantly got up to leave. "I wish I could spend the day with you, but I have to work half a day, and then I am going to touch base with the caterer."

The family resemblance of Mary and Abigail was noticeable. Mary's light brown hair was long and fastened away from her face with barrettes. Abigail's hair was a shade darker and woven into a thick braid. Both women had blue-gray eyes and a fair complexion.

Karin was curious about Abigail's work. "We heard that you were attending a woman in labor last night."

"Yes, it was her second baby and her labor this time was just four hours. Beautiful baby boy. Mom and baby are doing well," Abigail said with a smile. "Mary told me that you are a labor and delivery nurse."

"Yes. Northland Hospital doesn't have any midwives. Our doctors don't want to work with midwives. Do you have a physician back-up?"

"I work with Dr. Larson. He's an obstetrician. He takes over if there are complications. And he handles the patients that need to be induced or want an epidural. My practice centers on women that want natural childbirth. Then I assist them in working with their labor."

"Do you mean that all of your patients go through labor without pain medication?" Karin said.

"Pain isn't all bad. It helps a woman tune in to her body, change position, and assist the baby's descent in the birth canal."

"Okay, okay, enough shop talk," Mary said. She knew that Abigail could get into a long discussion on maternal health.

"Mary, did Karin tell you that her grandmother grew up on a farm in this area?" Jenny said.

"No way," Mary said. She turned to Karin, "When did you find that out?"

"When I went to Florida for her funeral. She was going to be buried in a cemetery somewhere around Calumet. How far is Calumet from Mine Harbor?"

"It's the next town, less than ten miles away. There is a big cemetery that overlooks Lake Superior." Mary said.

"What was her name?" Abigail asked.

"Marja Maki."

"That's definitely a Finnish name," Mary said. "You never mentioned her."

Karin blushed. "I learned a lot of things I didn't know at her funeral."

"I'm sorry. It's hard to lose family," Mary said.

There was an awkward pause, and then Abigail turned to Jenny, "What about you, Jenny? What kind of degree do you have?" Abigail asked.

"I'm a nurse also. I'm getting some basic experience working on a medical-surgical floor."

"I guess I'm the only non-medical person in this group," Mary said.

Karin almost reminded Mary that Lori was non-medical, and then pushed the thought away.

The conversation shifted to Mary's honeymoon and plans to move to Indiana. "Jason starts classes in January at Purdue. In the meantime, the Larsons have a duplex that they have offered to us for a couple of months. This means we can be near family for the holidays. In Indiana we will be living in graduate student housing, and I'll look for a job."

The girls finished their breakfast and cleaned off the dining room table; then Mary brought out a stack of programs. "We need to assemble the pages and tie ribbons on these."

"Do you have any Tylenol?" Karin said. "My neck and shoulders are still sore."

"Sure, I'll get it." Mary went to the kitchen.

"I know just the treatment for you. My dad was planning to heat the sauna today. We could all go for a sauna. Mary, what do you think?" Abigail said.

"Well, I'd like to get the programs done. I should check with Jason about the evening. Let me call him."

Mary made a brief phone call. Jason was working on putting a video together for the reception and encouraged her to go ahead with the sauna plans.

Abigail went right to the phone and called her mom. She explained her plan and then said, "No problem, we can help." She hung up the phone and turned to the girls. "We should have time to get the programs done. We need to head out to my home around four o'clock. The sauna won't be ready until five or six, but we can help my mom prepare vegetables for the soup she's making."

"Okay, let's get started," Mary said.

The girls settled at the dining room table. Jenny looked over the materials and said, "Two of us can assemble programs, and the other two can cut ribbons and tie them."

"Abigail and I will assemble them if you and Karin can do the ribbons," Mary said.

"I'd rather assemble," Jenny said. "My bows never turn out right."

"Okay, help me assemble. Abigail can you tie bows?"

"Sure."

The girls worked with intensity, and the time flew by. They stopped for a quick lunch break and continued. They were able to finish the programs and begin organizing decorations that they would bring to the church. It was Karin that noticed the time. "Wow, it's already four o'clock."

Mary looked at the stack of completed programs. "Thank-you so much! I'll leave my mom a note. Let's pack up some clean clothes and get going. Abigail, do we need to take towels?"

"No, we have plenty."

Karin and Jenny had been limited in their view of the Aaltio farm when they arrived the night before. Nor had they taken much time to view their surroundings in the morning. The farm was on the homestead site that Abigail's ancestor had claimed and cleared when he came from Finland. The house was back from the road with fields extending behind it. The original structure had been expanded, enlarging the kitchen and adding a family room.

Several other buildings dotted the property. The weathered brown barn was still standing. The sauna was a separate building in back of the house. The original sauna where John Aaltio's grandfather had been born was gone. The current sauna had been there as long as Mary and Abigail could remember.

"You will see—you will feel so good. My dad heats the sauna every Saturday and occasionally during the week. When we were growing up we frequently had potluck dinners, and our families would take saunas. The women and girls would take a sauna first, and then the men and boys would go. It was part of our preparation for Sunday," Abigail explained.

The girls went in the house and found Abigail's mother busy in the kitchen. A large stockpot was steaming on the stove, sending an aroma of chicken, onions, and herbs into the air. Potatoes and carrots were set out on the counter. Mrs. Aaltio welcomed the girls. "I was hoping you would take advantage of the sauna before the wedding. Here, help me with the carrots and potatoes. Peel and dice them. We'll add them to the soup. You can have cold cider, soup, and some bread I baked today—after your sauna."

Abigail said, "Karin and I can peel. Mary and Jenny can do the dicing." The girls set to it and had the task done in no time. Abigail brought a stack of towels, washcloths, and two types of shampoo and conditioner.

"Everyone grab a towel, washcloth, and your clean clothes. Let's head out to the sauna."

A path worn in the grass led from the house to the sauna. The sauna door opened to a dressing room that had hooks on the wall for clothes, a shelf for toiletries, and a wooden bench against one wall. Once inside the dressing room, Abigail opened another door. "This is the shower room, and the door at the side of the shower room opens to the actual sauna. Dad has kept a fire going in the stove all afternoon."

Abigail and Mary began to undress. Jenny blushed and said, "So we all get undressed and do this bath thing together—uh, naked?"

Mary started. "We're so used to going to the sauna we don't think twice about being naked. You can wear a towel if you like. There are some extra ones."

Karin and Jenny undressed and grabbed towels. The girls tiptoed across the shower room and opened the door to the adjacent room. A waft of hot air greeted them. As they entered, Abigail warned them to stay clear of the stove on the right side of the room. The iron stove gave evidence of the wood fire burning inside by the glowing color that peeked through the edge of the stove door. The top of it was covered with large, smooth stones. Over a period of hours, the stones and the walls of the room had absorbed heat from the fire that Abigail's father had stoked periodically. The room was radiant with heat and the scent of cedar. The stones were sizzling hot.

On the left side of the room were two wooden benches built into the sauna wall. The first was the level of a regular seat; the second was about two feet higher and narrower in width. A bunch of fresh cedar branches, tied in a whisk, lay on the lower bench.

"It's a good idea to start out by sitting on the lower bench, and then move up to the top bench if you want more heat," explained Abigail.

For a few minutes they all sat on the lower bench. Abigail took a dipper of warm water from a pail she had filled when they entered the sauna room. She threw the water on the hot stones, and hissing steam arose. The girls could feel the mist as they took a breath in.

Abigail handed Karin and Jenny wet washcloths. "If you want, you can put a wash cloth over your face to cool the steam."

The moist heat felt good to Karin. It was loosening the muscles in her neck and shoulders in a comforting way. Karin picked up the whisk of cedar branches. "What is this for?"

"Mary, you show her," Abigail suggested. Mary smiled and took the cedar branches. She spanked her arms, legs, and back with the branches.

"It stimulates the circulation," Mary said, responding to Karin's puzzled look.

Mary and Abigail moved to the upper bench. The women relaxed in the cleansing steam. Abigail threw another dipper of water on the rocks. Jenny had her head down. "I don't think I can take much more."

"Time to go out and shower," Abigail instructed. Jenny left the sauna room, and as soon as she finished her shower, Karin followed.

Twenty minutes later Abigail and Mary emerged from the sauna room and took their showers. Jenny and Karin were already dressed. Karin said, "I can't believe you stayed in there so long!"

"Oh, we're used to it. We just douse ourselves with a pail of cool water and then take a little more steam. So what do you think of an authentic sauna?" Mary asked, her face glowing.

"The heat was really strong—especially when Abigail tossed the water. But I can truthfully say, I have never felt so clean and relaxed." Karin glanced at Mary. "A pretty good way to prepare for your wedding night."

Jenny giggled and then asked Mary. "Are you and Jason still waiting for the wedding night?" She knew that Mary had avoided having sex during college. Karin raised her eyebrows. She would not ask such a direct question, but she was curious. She had given in to a boyfriend during her college years and then regretted it. But if she was really in love it might be different.

Mary was flushed from the heat of the sauna. If she blushed, it was impossible to tell. She paused and searched for words. "It gets hard to wait—I'm a little nervous about what it will be like. But we are committed to waiting until we are married."

"What difference does it make?" Jenny asked. "You're going to get married."

"The most important part of our relationship is our commitment to each other. We want to do that first," Mary said.

Jenny and Karin were aware that Mary relied on the Bible for direction in her life. They were often surprised by her viewpoints and her ability to talk about her decisions. Mary and Jason shared convictions and had an unusual respect for each other.

Mary is lucky, Karin thought.

During dinner, Karin and Jenny met Abigail's brothers, Paul and Ray. Paul was taking classes at Finlandia University in Hancock. Ray was still in high school.

They learned that Mr. Aaltio taught Finnish language and literature at Paul's college. He was working on a book about the history and culture of the Finnish sauna. He described the old smoke saunas and how the original ventilation methods allowed smoke to escape from small vents along the eaves or from a sliding opening in the door. After the fire had burned for most of the day, it was allowed to go out. The smoke dissipated, but the rocks and walls remained thoroughly heated. The process left the sauna room clean and free of bacteria. It was the cleanest place for birthing babies and for treating illness. In the old days, a family built a sauna first and then the house.

"Many Finnish babies were born in the sauna," John Aaltio explained.

"How did that work?" Karin asked. "Did a doctor come to the sauna?"

"When my great-grandmother gave birth, she had a midwife," Abigail said. "When her labor went on for more than a day they sent for the doctor but the midwife delivered the baby before the doctor could get there. Right, Dad?"

"That's right," John said.

Karin tried to wrap her mind around the idea of birth in a sauna. It sounded dangerous and scary. Everything in the hospital was carefully monitored.

John continued, "The sauna was central to Finnish families. It was a place of relaxation and cleanliness in harsh environments. It had both physical and emotional effects; the tranquility of the sauna room provided relief from stress."

"I feel like I have stepped back in time," Karin said.

"The sauna is a cherished part of family memories for me," Mary said.

"Well, Mary, are you going to ask Jason to build a sauna?" Jenny asked.

Mary laughed. "Oh, I would love to have a sauna. Otherwise we'll come back and visit Uncle John and Aunt Rita." Rita asked about the wedding preparations, and the girls mentioned the programs and the activities for the next day. They planned to spend the morning decorating the church reception room and the afternoon relaxing before the rehearsal.

The day of the wedding was crisp and clear, a few puffy white clouds dotting the sky. The wedding was to be at noon, but the wedding party arrived at the church in advance. The stained glass windows of the church shimmered in the sunshine, and the dark wood steeple pointing heavenward was distinct against the blue sky.

Mary and her attendants entered the frame church building and headed for a classroom where they would dress. The photographer was coming at 11:00 a.m. to take pictures of the bride and her bridesmaids. He would also take some family pictures and pictures of the groom separately. Mary did not want Jason to see her until she walked down the aisle.

Mary's mom and Abigail assisted her in putting on her gown. It was a soft and lustrous ivory silk with simple lines. The neckline was embellished with delicate embroidery and beads. Mary's hair was partially pinned back, and a cascade of light brown curls flowed along her neck. Abigail helped pin her veil in place.

Abigail, Karin, and Jenny were wearing peach-colored dresses, fitted at the waist. The skirt was full and mid-calf length. The dress accentuated Karin's lithesome figure. Her fair coloring and dark brown hair rounded out a very pretty look, but she did not outshine the bride.

Mary looked radiant, and her attendants enjoyed being in her sunshine. She was the first of their circle of friends to move on to marriage.

"You know the saying . . . 'Something old, something new, something borrowed, something blue,'" Abigail said. "I have something old. Here's a penny with the same year as Jason's birthday. Slip it in your shoe."

Karin produced a lace handkerchief. "You can borrow this and put it around the handle of your bouquet." Karin was giving way to a little sentimentality. The warmth of Mary and Abigail's family was a tonic.

Jenny sighed. She was going along with this old-fashioned rite. "You still need something blue." She held out a package of Lifesavers mints. "They're blue and they're new." That broke the tension, and they all laughed. Mary opened the Lifesavers and passed them around.

There were tears in Mary's eyes as she gazed at her friends. "You are dear. I am lucky to have such good friends." She glanced at Karin—they both remembered Lori. Mary caught Karin's hand and squeezed it.

There was a tap at the classroom door, and Mary's mom opened the door. Karin and Jenny were dumbstruck as they gazed at the young man with a camera.

"What is he doing here?" Jenny asked.

The handsome young man smiled and said, "Hello ladies. I guess we meet again."

Mary looked puzzled. "Do you know Peter?"

"He rescued us. He tied down the hood of my car!" Karin said.

"So he was your good Samaritan! That's wild. Well, let me introduce Peter Janson. Peter is a good friend of my brother and has agreed to be our photographer," Mary explained. "Peter, this is Jenny and Karin, my roommates from college."

"Thank-you for your help. I don't think we adequately expressed our thanks," Jenny said as she extended her hand.

Peter accepted her hand. "Glad to help."

Peter held out his hand to Karin and their eyes met. "I'm pleased to meet you," Karin said. This time she noticed his striking hazel eyes and the gentle lines of his face. "I'm glad we have another chance to thank you. So you're a photographer?"

"I do some freelance photography. Can't quite make it my full-time job," he said with a broad smile. He thought Karin looked stunning. Was it the dress, her fair coloring or her deep brown eyes that attracted him? "Well, let's get started."

After taking a few shots in the classroom, he led the group to the sanctuary. He directed Mary and her attendants in front of the altar, adjusting their positions and snapping picture after picture.

The guests had begun to arrive when Abigail, Karin, and Jenny led Mary out the side door from the front of the sanctuary and back to the classroom. They watched the clock, and a couple of minutes before noon, they filed out to the church foyer.

The music changed to "Trumpet Voluntary" and Jenny began her walk down the aisle, first in the bridal procession. Karin followed her and concentrated on walking in rhythm to the music. High heel shoes were a nuisance. She frowned with worry that she might trip over her feet.

She sighed with relief when she reached the altar and turned to watch Abigail and then Mary come down the aisle.

Jason and Mary repeated their vows with steady voices. The couple knelt for prayer after lighting the unity candle. When the pastor announced Jason and Mary as man and wife, they turned to face their family and friends with glowing faces.

The reception hall was decorated with bouquets of mums in shades of gold and copper. A video monitor ran a constant loop of pictures of Mary and Jason. Guests found seats at tables covered in white linen. A buffet table featured smoked fish, ham, potato and beet salad, fresh baked rolls, *juustoleipä*, and pastries. Family and friends enjoyed fellowship, took pictures, and celebrated the couple. Peter was busy photographing much of the time but took a short break after the wedding cake was cut.

Noticing an empty chair next to Karin, he paused. He caught her glance, "Mind if I sit here?"

"It's okay with me—are you going to get some wedding cake?"

"Good idea," Peter put his camera on the table and came back with coffee and cake.

"Is this your first trip to the UP?" Peter asked.

"What do you mean?" Karin asked.

Peter laughed. "The Upper Peninsula of Michigan—the UP. I guess this is your first time here."

"Yes, whole new experience. How long have you lived here?"

"Since attending Michigan Tech. Finished school and the place grew on me. I decided to stay," Peter said.

"You said that you do photography on the side. Do you have another job?"

"I work in IT at Michigan Tech—keep their computers running." Before Peter could elaborate, Jenny waved and motioned for Karin to come. Karin loitered a moment before Jenny walked over to the table and said, "Hurry, Mary and Jason are getting ready to leave. We're going out to the church steps."

Karin and Peter got up and followed Jenny outside. Peter had his camera ready as they joined the group blowing bubbles and waiting for Mary and Jason. The newlyweds waved as they ran down the church steps to their car. As the guests dispersed, Karin looked for Peter but didn't see him anywhere.

The day after the wedding, Karin got directions to Lakeview Cemetery from Abigail. Jenny went with Karin and they drove down the main street of Calumet. The buildings were old, some dating back to 1900. Gift shops, a sporting goods store, and a hardware store were housed in buildings that had once contained other businesses. There were a couple of restaurants and an art gallery. When the mines had been at peak performance, there had been numerous saloons and bars catering to the miners.

They turned down a residential street that connected to the highway. They drove by old two-story homes, which had been built by the Calumet and Hecla Mining Company. The frame homes had enclosed porches, and some had new siding. Others were worn and tired looking.

"It seems like time has stopped here," Jenny mused.

"It tugs at my heart. I would like to know more about the people who once lived here," Karin said. She thought about her grandmother. Now that she was gone, Karin thought about the many questions she wanted to ask.

She wanted to know more about her mother's side of the family and this grandmother who had been praying for her. What had life in this town been like years ago? When did she leave?

The highway took them outside of town to a view of trees clothed in shades of red, ocher, gold, and burnt orange. Karin drove slowly, pausing to look at trees on both sides of the road. Before long they saw the entrance to Lakeview marked with brick pillars. Karin parked next to the caretaker's office and went in to inquire about the location of Marja Maki's grave.

"It's a good thing you asked for directions," Jenny remarked as Karin got back in the car. "This cemetery is huge."

They drove down the center driveway and then made a right turn. They crossed a couple of paths. The names on the gravestones gave an international flavor to the cemetery. They noticed Italian, Polish, German, Swedish, and French names on the markers.

"I think this is the section," Karin said as she parked. The air was crisp, cool, and invigorating as the girls stepped out. A light mist in the air gave a clue to the nearness of Lake Superior.

"This gravestone is really old. Can you read it?" Karin asked Jenny.

Jenny bent down and studied the worn lettering. "Belle Hooper. Looks like she was born in 1862 and died in 1910."

They came across a lot of Finnish names: Palosaari, Hyvonen, Ojala. Eventually they found Arvo and Marja Maki's gravestone. Near their marker was a stone with barely visible lettering.

"Father Eino Maki, 1881 to 1937. Mother Elsa Maki, 1885 to 1952. I guess they would be my great-grandparents."

"Do you know what your grandmother's maiden name was?"

"No . . ."

"If you did, we could look for her family's site," Jenny said.

"You know, I have this case of stuff that was given to me after the funeral. But I haven't opened it. So much was going on. Now I'm curious about what's in it."

Chapter 5

M RS. SANDER CAME to Chicago for a weekend, and Karin helped her pack up Lori's belongings. As they sorted, they wept and shared memories. Each framed photograph touched a nerve. In one photograph, Karin and Lori were grinning, arms draped around each other in their high school graduation gowns. "Lori was so happy that day," Mrs. Sander said.

Mrs. Sander kept photographs, jewelry, and a couple of books. She gave Karin a gold necklace with an opal pendant. Karin accepted it reluctantly. It seemed strange to be packing up emblems of Lori's life. They donated the majority of Lori's belongings to a resale shop that benefited a women's shelter.

After Mrs. Sander left, Karin finished cleaning Lori's room. When she moved the bed around to vacuum, she found a medication container that had rolled beneath. She picked it up and glanced at the label curiously. Misoprostol. The name of the medication sounded familiar, but she couldn't place it. What was Lori being treated for?

Karin looked for the other pill container. She pulled out a notebook and wrote down the date that the misoprostol was prescribed, the date that the Tylenol with codeine was prescribed, and the date that Lori died. It was a timeline that contained a revelation. Karin wondered if Jenny was at home. She needed to talk with someone.

Jenny answered the phone. "Can you figure out who prescribed her medications?" Jenny asked.

"The same doctor's name is on both labels, but I don't recognize the name, and I don't have any way of knowing where he practices," Karin said.

"It had to be a clinic or urgent care facility," Jenny said.

"Maybe if I had known what was going on, I could have given information in the emergency room," Karin said.

"Don't go there. You did what you could," Jenny said.

"But here's the thing, she told me that she called the doctor and got a prescription. It sounds like he gave her pain pills without seeing her."

"You know, I have been thinking about coming to Chicago. It would be easy for me to take the train again. Can I hang out with you? I'm off next weekend," Jenny said.

"Well, sure. That would be great." Karin welcomed the idea of company. The apartment was lonely.

The following evening Karin was sitting at the nurses' station keeping an eye on the monitor screen. The nurses' station was like a command center with telephones, computers, and medication dispensers. The monitor showed input from eight labor rooms. Each room was represented by a square that contained a graph of contractions and a tracing of the baby's heart rate. Karin was focusing on two rooms. She watched the frequency of the contractions and the baby's response to the contractions.

Karin noticed the strong musk scent of a man's cologne and felt a hand on her shoulder. Dr. Cutter spoke up from behind her. "What's the pitocin at for my patient?"

"She's at eight milli-units."

"Keep going up. We need to get her delivered." Dr. Cutter didn't name a time, but Karin knew that he wanted to deliver his patient by 9:00 p.m. It was a part of time management. This meticulously organized doctor did gyne surgery in the morning, had office hours in the afternoon, and liked to plan deliveries for the evening. His message was brief, and he left the nurses' station, leather shoes clacking down the hall.

He worked at the hospital Monday through Thursday. He seldom appeared on the weekend. If one of his patients needed urgent care on those days, another doctor covered for him.

Dr. Cutter liked to schedule his patients for induced labor when they reached thirty-nine weeks gestation. Sometimes he placed a medication in the vagina to soften the cervix. Sometimes he prescribed pitocin, to be given in an intravenous drip. Dr. Cutter encouraged women to choose the time that they would give birth and gave a brief sketch of the interventions involved.

For each labor induction Karin and her colleagues carefully watched the pitocin level, the contractions, and the baby's response. The fetal heart rate tracing provided information about the baby's well being. Epidural anesthesia was offered to provide relief from pain.

The labor rooms were furnished like comfortable bedrooms. As the woman's labor progressed, monitor cords, blinking digital read-outs with alarms, intravenous tubes, and urinary catheters appeared one by one from camouflaged cabinets. The laboring woman was attached to the fetal monitor, an intravenous pump, and eventually an epidural pump. The epidural limited her movement in bed due to loss of muscle strength in her legs. Because she was unable to sense her bladder filling up, she required a urinary catheter.

Labor had to be carefully managed. A drop in blood pressure in response to epidural anesthesia affected blood flow to the baby. This was corrected with intravenous fluids and medication.

Despite aggressive management, sometimes labor stalled. The technical approach to birth limited position changes, movement of legs and pelvis that assist the baby to move down the vaginal passageway. The remedy was higher doses of pitocin, more contractions with less rest between contractions. If the baby didn't tolerate this management of labor the woman was moved to the operating room for a cesarean section.

On rare occasions a true emergency occurred—a placental abruption that caused heavy bleeding, a seizure caused by toxemia, or a sudden drop in the baby's heart rate without recovery. When these problems were diagnosed, the staff pulled together with an adrenaline rush and moved the patient to the operating room quickly.

Dr. Cutter returned around 8:30 p.m. and Karin accompanied him to his patient's room. On examining the patient and finding that she was nine centimeters dilated, he explained that she could start pushing soon. He instructed Karin to check her again in fifteen minutes and to position her for pushing.

At 9:00 p.m. he returned, and Karin was coaching the patient with pushing. She was standing next to the patient urging her to push hard and then encouraging her to relax at the end of the contraction. The volume on the fetal monitor was turned up, and the sound of the baby's heartbeat thumped in the background like a galloping horse.

Dr. Cutter examined the patient again. He said to the patient, "I want you to push harder. Do you see this graph of your contractions?" He pointed to the digital screen. "The toco pressure is eighty. I want you to increase the pressure to a hundred. Okay now, push, push harder!"

Dr. Cutter coached the patient through a couple more contractions and then said, "I can help you out. The baby's head is low, and I can put a little vacuum on the baby's head and assist your push."

He turned to Karin. "Put her legs in stirrups and get me the vacuum extractor." Karin did as he asked and made sure the baby warmer was ready with the suction tubing and oxygen set-up ready to go.

Dr. Cutter said to the patient, "I want you to listen to me and do exactly what I tell you to do. I will tell you when to push and when to stop." He applied the vacuum extractor to the baby's head and asked the patient to push.

Dr. Cutter pulled the baby with the vacuum extractor as the woman pushed. "Keep pushing, keep pushing . . . now take a breath. Okay, push again." The baby's head emerged and then the rest of the body. Dr. Cutter held the baby up before placing him on the woman's chest.

Karin stood by as the woman gazed at her baby and cuddled him for a minute. Then she took him over to the warmer. The nursery nurse dried him off completely and did a quick assessment of his color, breathing, respiration, and muscle tone.

After delivery of the placenta, Karin made sure the intravenous fluid with pitocin was running. Dr. Cutter was in the habit of giving extra medication to insure that the uterus contracted, after being stimulated with pitocin. Sometimes the uterus was tired after a long induction. He asked Karin for Cytotec. Karin called the nurse's station and asked one of her colleagues to bring 400 micrograms of Cytotec.

Karin looked at the medication packet before opening it for Dr. Cutter. The label read misoprostol. Karin froze. The generic name for Cytotec was misoprostol. Lori had taken misoprostol. Why?

"Karin, please open the Cytotec." Dr. Cutter said loudly and that snapped Karin back to the present. She opened the packet and dropped the tiny pills into Dr. Cutter's hand. He inserted them into the patient's rectum. The pills stimulated the smooth muscle of the uterus to contract.

Dr. Cutter was anxious to complete this case and ready to begin stitching the episiotomy he had done to speed up the delivery. His glasses had slipped down his nose, and he couldn't adjust them because he was keeping his gloved hands sterile. He called to Karin to fix his glasses. She suppressed a smile. It seemed like she had to fix his glasses with every delivery.

When Dr. Cutter was done, Karin began recovery care for the patient. She checked the uterus for firmness and checked vital signs. When Karin was sure that her patient was stable, she gave the baby to the mother. The husband was standing by and she left the room, allowing bonding time for the new family.

Karin was finishing up her documentation at the nurses' station when Dr. Cutter came out to the desk. "You seem a little out of it, Karin. Everything okay?"

"I lost my roommate. She died and I'm living alone in the apartment. I can barely pay my rent. What can I say?" It was unlike Karin to spout personal problems, but fatigue and stress had worn down her reserve.

"Damn, that's a load. What happened to your roommate?"

Karin told him the story that she was still processing. Dr. Cutter shook his head. "That is really tragic," he said. Then he came over and massaged her shoulders.

Karin mentioned the medication containers that she had found.

"It just seems so strange that she could get so sick and die. She was in the hospital, and they couldn't save her. They said she had a raging infection and died of septicemia."

"I'm really sorry, Karin," Dr. Cutter said.

Dr. Dylan Cutter carried himself with confidence and it gave his average height the appearance of greater stature. The scent of cologne was always strong about his person. His black hair was slicked back with styling gel. His wire-rimmed glasses shaded gray eyes. His glasses tended to slip down his thin, straight nose, and he often paused to push them up.

He made a point of befriending nurses. He wanted women to appreciate him. Karin knew that he was recently divorced. She wondered what his wife had been like.

When Dr. Cutter asked Karin if she would like to meet him for a drink after work, she paused before giving a reply. What would it hurt? Just a drink. She wanted a break from her lonely apartment.

It was midnight when she left work and headed to Bailey's Bar and Grill across the street. She entered the restaurant and looked around; Dr. Cutter was not in sight. She waited fifteen minutes and was about to leave when he came through the door.

"Sorry, a couple of things came up. Let's get a drink." He led her to a table, and they ordered beer and nachos. They made small talk about the events of the day and the hospital politics. Dylan adjusted his glasses. After a period of silence, he asked Karin if she was planning to take on a new roommate.

"I need to have a new roommate, but I'm not sure how I'll go about it. I keep expecting Lori to walk through the door."

Dr. Cutter encouraged Karin to talk about Lori. He asked her full name and about her interests. Karin was relieved to talk with someone who was willing to listen to her memories. The pent up thoughts streamed out. Dr. Cutter listened with a question here and there. Later Karin couldn't remember what she had said.

On her next day off, Karin decided to pursue investigation of Lori's prescriptions. She called the pharmacy phone number on the label of the bottle. She gave the prescription number and the name of the prescribing doctor, Dr. Smith.

"I am hoping to locate this doctor. Can you tell me where Dr. Smith practices?" Karin asked.

"No, ma'am, I can't," the pharmacy tech responded.

"It is important that I find him," Karin said.

"Sorry, I don't have that information."

Jenny arrived mid-morning on Friday. Karin almost didn't recognize her as passengers disembarked from the train. Her long red hair had been cropped short. With mousse or gel she had styled it in little spikes. "Wow, Jenny!"

Jenny pivoted. "Like my new do?" Karin grinned and Jenny said, "I was ready for a change."

They discussed plans for the weekend, and Jenny listened to Karin's musings. "I wish I had my laptop with me. Where can we find a computer? If we could do a computer search on misoprostol we might find something."

"I use the computer at the library," Karin said. "It's not far from here. Let's go."

Both women gasped when RU–486 came up in their quest. Misoprostol is the second medication used in the treatment that is known as RU–486. The first medication is given at a medical office or abortion clinic. Misoprostol follows the first medication and although it is supposed to be closely monitored, some clinics give it to the patient to take at home.

"Lori must have been pregnant and getting an abortion," Jenny said. Her voice was flat.

Karin's head was reeling. The pieces of Lori's last week started to fit. Lori had broken up with Mike. Karin had noticed many saturated menstrual pads in the bathroom trash. The pain pills.

"Oh my gosh, poor Lori," Karin said. "Lori's death certificate says that she died of septicemia; it might have started with an abortion. We need to find out who prescribed the pills, where she was treated."

"That won't be an easy task given the HIPAA rules. But I guess we could check out abortion clinics," Jenny said. They looked up abortion clinics on the Internet and decided to visit a couple.

The first clinic they visited was located in a strip mall. The face of the building was nondescript. They checked the address and walked up to the door. The clinic appeared to be open but the door was locked.

Jenny noticed the doorbell, "It says to press the bell and then speak into the intercom." She read the sign. "Tell us if you are dropping off supplies or if you have an appointment."

"What should I say?" Karin was thinking out loud. While Karin and Jenny stood there, a woman exited. Jenny caught the door.

"Come on," she said as she pulled Karin inside. When they approached the reception desk a young woman asked if they had an appointment.

"No," Karin replied. "We were wondering if we might speak with Dr. Smith. A friend of ours was treated by him."

The young woman shook her head.

"Is he here?" Jenny asked.

"Look, I don't know why you are here. You can't just barge into a clinic and expect to see a doctor. If you want to see a doctor, you need to call and make an appointment."

"Can you tell us if Lori Sander was treated at this clinic?" Karin asked.

"There is no Dr. Smith here, and we don't give out information about our patients. I think you had better leave or I will call our security guard."

Jenny looked at Karin and nodded with her head toward the door. "Let's go."

When they got outside, Karin said, "Well, that didn't get us anywhere."

Shortly after the young women left, the receptionist picked up the phone and paged Dr. Smith. When he called back, she said, "Something strange just happened. Two women came in asking questions about a Lori Sander. They also asked if you worked at this clinic. Out of curiosity I checked our files, and I found records for Lori Sander."

"What did you tell them?"

"I told them that we don't give out information. I also said that there is no Dr. Smith here."

"Good girl. You did exactly the right thing. When a girl has an abortion there are always snoops who want to find out about it." Dr. Smith wondered if it was the same case that Dylan had mentioned to him. He wasn't sure. He made a mental note to go over the medical record.

Karin and Jenny drove to the next address but were unable to gain entrance there. They went back to Karin's apartment and decided to make phone calls to the clinics.

The phone calls were not successful. "We should have expected this," Jenny said. "We have the HIPAA rules in the hospital. It's not surprising that the abortion clinics are even tighter with their information. What if we did a search for Dr. Smith? Where is your phone book?"

Aliisa's Letter

"I don't have one—I just have a cell phone and never got a Chicago phone book. Besides what would we say—how can we get any information from a doctor's office?" Karin questioned.

After a period of silence, Jenny agreed that they had come to an impasse. They spent the evening making plans for the next day. The rest of the weekend went by quickly. Jenny was enthralled with the shopping in Chicago. "You have the best stores here. And next time I come I'd like to go to the Art Institute." Before she headed home she took down the names of a couple of hospitals where she might like to work. "I'll work on getting an Illinois nursing license," she said. "You need a roommate."

Chapter 6

BIGAIL HAD MADE her decision to practice in Mine Harbor after spending time abroad. She had graduated from the midwifery program at Marquette University and spent a year at a mission hospital in Africa. The hospital was an outpost in an area that had no other medical care available. With limited resources she had provided prenatal care and delivered babies at the hospital, coping with unreliable electric power. She learned skills to avoid a cesarean section if at all possible.

When she came home from Africa, she had chosen to stay in Michigan because of its favorable climate for midwifery. Some states made it very difficult for midwives to practice. Abigail's father recommended that she talk to Dr. Larson.

Dr. Ben Larson was an old friend of John Aaltio. They had gone to high school together, but John went to Suomi College and Ben had gone to the University of Michigan. After medical school he went to Chicago for his residency. He eventually joined a large practice in the nearby suburbs. At first, he was fascinated by the high-risk cases and the technology available. Over time, however, he had become disenchanted.

Lawsuits and the high cost of malpractice insurance forced him to re-evaluate his goals.

When Ben went back to Mine Harbor for a visit, friends told him that the older doctors were retiring. And it was hard to attract new doctors to the Upper Peninsula. They were looking for family practice doctors and an obstetrician. The regional hospital in Hancock and the little hospital in Mine Harbor were recruiting. It was perfect timing. Even though he was taking a substantial cut in pay, Ben left the high-pressure practice in Illinois and returned to his roots.

Dr. Larson had been back in Mine Harbor for a year when Abigail wrote him a letter, listing her credentials and expressing her desire to practice there. Ben read the letter and put it down with consternation. He had never worked with a midwife. But this was John's daughter. His wife suggested they invite Abigail over for dinner.

Ben and Evelyn lived in a two-story frame duplex. Evelyn had overseen the remodeling and refurbishing of their home. The old hardwood floors, door frames, and moldings had been stripped and refinished. The wood shone and brought warmth into the rooms. The curtains, sofa, and chairs were in shades of green, lavender and pink. Evelyn had made the old house into a home and the adjoining house was a bonus.

Evelyn was a gifted hostess. She enjoyed putting together a menu and delighted in conversation over a good meal. The dining room was filled with the aroma of freshly baked rolls and roast sirloin of beef seasoned with rosemary, thyme, and onions. The scent of the herbs was soothing and enticing.

Evelyn had lots of herbs growing in the sunroom. At one time a pantry, the room faced south. New, larger windows had been put in, and two grow lights had been installed above a narrow table. During the long winter months it was necessary to augment sunlight to sustain the plants. The table provided space for herbs and seedlings for the summer garden.

The adjustment to northern Michigan had been difficult for Evelyn. She left long-term friendships and a job teaching literature for a community college. She had been involved in women's ministries at her church. In Mine Harbor, she invested time in learning about the community by attending local events. And she put energy into gardening and cooking.

A forest green tablecloth covered the dining room table. White dinner plates were adorned with lime green napkins, carefully folded. Antique etched water glasses were filled with ice water. Evelyn had just set out the hot meal for Ben, Abigail, and herself.

Ben was dressed in a flannel shirt and wrinkled slacks. His gray hair was a little shaggy. He had kicked back to more casual attire since making the move to Mine Harbor. His personality style and rugged appearance were reminiscent of a sheriff on the western frontier. His relaxed appearance contrasted with Evelyn's neat and stylish dress. He had a direct gaze that invited conversation and put people at ease.

Ben asked Abigail about the program at Marquette University. Abigail summarized her experience in the hospital and clinic settings. "Birth is absolutely amazing. I enjoy working with a woman through her labor. But most of all I enjoy teaching women about their bodies. Pregnancy, labor, and birth tend to be healthy if a woman takes good care of her body."

Ben smiled, impressed by her passion. He explained, "The delivery rate at Harbor Hospital is nowhere near the numbers of a big city hospital. My practice may have anywhere from five to fifteen births per month."

"I might draw additional patients. Some women are looking for a midwife," Abigail said.

Ben Larson gazed thoughtfully at Abigail. He knew that improved education for women led to better infant health. He just didn't have the time to do it well. He had revised his perspective on maternal and infant health since leaving Chicago.

Evelyn caught his eye and gave him a little nod. Ben could read Evelyn's approval of Abigail. She was signaling a yes vote.

"If you want to join me, this is what I am thinking. I will need help with routine physicals, office visits. We will attend some births together, and eventually you can cover normal births. I will take care of complicated pregnancies and gynecological problems. After a few months, I will evaluate our teamwork."

By the time Evelyn served dessert, Ben and Abigail had come to an understanding. Abigail was going to join Dr. Larson's practice, at least temporarily.

Ben took Abigail on a tour of the hospital the next day. She had come to the hospital's emergency room once as a child. She was pleased to come back as a health care provider. Abigail met a couple of the family practice physicians and a few nurses. She walked through the labor unit, composed of five labor-delivery-recovery-postpartum rooms or LDRPs.

When Karin checked her mail, she found two letters amid the junk mail. She opened a letter from Mary first. She scanned through the greeting and Mary's description of married life. A couple of sentences stood out. *Have you looked through the box of your grandmother's things? I'm curious to know what you found.*

At the end of Mary's letter was an invitation. *What are your plans for Thanksgiving? We'd love it if you could come for a long weekend or more!* Karin put the letter down. Could she do it? Could she make another long trip to Upper Michigan? It was a long drive, but she longed for the warmth of friendship she had experienced with Mary and her relatives.

Abigail had sent a friendly note. She made reference to her job, and the joy she had working with women. Karin read that statement twice. The birth of a baby was a happy event, but labor management at

Northland Hospital was pretty stressful. Abigail also invited Karin to visit over Thanksgiving.

Mary's question stirred her to pull out the case from her grandmother. She opened it and placed the contents one by one on the coffee table: a worn, black leather Bible, a couple of photograph albums, a little bundle of letters tied with a ribbon, some old postcards. She picked up one of the postcards. It had a picture of a colorful nosegay tied with ribbon and labeled, *A Friendship Bouquet*. She turned the card over; the handwriting was foreign. "Finnish?" she wondered. The other postcards had landscapes, caricatures of young people, and Christmas scenes. Some cards had messages written in pencil, others in black ink.

She picked up the Bible and thumbed through it carefully because the pages were thin and delicate to the touch. The Bible fell open to glossy pages in the center where a letter, written in Finnish, was tucked. The centerfold had a chart for listing genealogy. The first page was filled out in a neat script. Aliisa Ahonen and Jan Kaartinen were united in marriage on September 10, 1905. Who were Aliisa and Jan?

Karin turned the page and came to a list of births. Eight names were listed and among the names, second to last was Marja. After Marja was Leila. The adjacent page listed deaths. At the top of the list was Leila. Karin checked the dates and figured that she had died when she was just four months old.

The final page listed marriages. There it was. Marja Kaartinen married Arvo Maki in 1948. So Aliisa and Jan were her grandmother's parents. This was a record of her grandmother's family. She opened the worn and tattered album. As she scanned through, she found a picture of a young woman with a solemn expression. A wisp of hair had come loose from the gently pinned knot at the nape of her neck and curled against her cheek. The shadows under her eyes hinted at fatigue. She wore an apron and held a baby in her arms. A toddler clung to her skirt and three other children surrounded her. Each of the children were dressed neatly, their hair combed. This was Aliisa with her children. Was the baby Marja?

She picked up the newest photograph album. The first page had a wedding picture of Karin's mother and father. Karin studied her mother's face, her mind pulling at memories long buried. She turned the pages slowly and came to her own baby pictures. Among those pictures were Marja and Arvo, standing together and Arvo proudly holding her. Fuzzy memories of the quiet, gentle man moved in and out of focus.

She found a picture of a picnic. Karin's mother, Anne, was holding her, and Marja and Arvo were sitting next to them. Karin remembered the park. But where was her father? Perhaps he took the picture. It was strange. These pictures took her back to a time that seemed to belong to someone else.

Her life with her father had been quiet. Her paternal grandparents had been available to spend holidays with them but that was all. Her dad's brother rarely visited because he lived on the west coast. Her mother's relatives had faded from her life after the auto accident. She had a new curiosity about her mother's side of the family as she stared at the old photos in her lap.

As she began to put things back in the case, she noticed a folded slip of paper, separate from the other items. The logo at the top read *The Finnish Steamship Company*. It was a receipt dated 1902 with the amount of $35.00 listed. Karin held the slip of paper in her hand thoughtfully. It was too late to ask Grandma Maki the questions that came to mind now.

Chapter 7

Sunday, November 26, 1899, has passed as an important date in the annals of the passenger railway service of Calumet and the copper country, for it marks the arrival and departure of the first through passenger train between Chicago, the metropolis of the entire west, and Calumet, the metropolis of copperdom.

—*Copper Country Evening News*, November 27, 1899

ALIISA LISTENED TO her mother talk about the letter recently received. "Matti says that Aliisa should come to the Copper Island. He is sending money for her passage to America. The towns of Red Jacket and nearby Laurium need domestic help. There are plenty of jobs for maids and cooks."

Aliisa's father asked, "Who is going to help out here?"

He knew that their life was a fight for survival. Already one son had left for America. The farm needed everyone's hands to keep going. When he was away fishing or hunting, Aliisa helped keep the barn clean, shoveling the manure. She and her mother took care of the animals, making sure they were fed and even assisting the cows with difficult calving. In the summer they planted the vegetable garden while he plowed and planted the rye. Aliisa and her mother foraged for wild berries and brought the animals to pasture.

Aliisa's mother said, "What kind of future does our daughter have here? We have survived starvation but the crops may fail again. Most of the young men are gone. They either have been conscripted into the Russian army or have found a way to get to America."

She was pained by the idea of letting her youngest daughter leave Finland, but she hoped Aliisa would find a better life in America.

Aliisa knew that it meant leaving relatives and the only community she had ever known, but she pushed this thought from her mind. She was excited about meeting Matti in America. She wanted to go to the place called Copper Island.

"Please let me go. I can earn money for you to come someday."

Aliisa's father frowned, but her mother supported her desire to go. Aliisa's first task was to get a letter of reference from the pastor of her parish, attesting to her character and her ability to read and write.

With the money Matti sent, Aliisa traveled to Oulu to get a passport and buy her passage from the Finnish Steamship Company. The Finnish Steamship Company gave her a booklet entitled, "Advice and Instructions to Travelers Going to America." This company arranged travel from Finland to England to the United States and then the train connections to Calumet, Michigan.

With the development of the copper mines in Michigan, there was a steady stream of emigrants traveling to the Upper Peninsula. The travel route was well established, and the steamship company provided guidance to Finnish travelers with a booklet in their own language.

In April of 1902, Aliisa left the port city of Oulu on the ship Polaris. Aliisa was traveling third class and followed the crowd of emigrants below deck. Although the capacity for third class passengers was 167, more than 300 emigrants were crowded below the deck. The first leg of their journey was to Hull, England, where they would be herded on a train to Liverpool. They would be given dormitory accommodations in Liverpool while they waited for their ship to depart.

Aliisa arrived in Liverpool with some trepidation but also the thrill of adventure. She linked up with a Finnish family who was also making the big trip to America. She could not have anticipated Liverpool. The sights and sounds were confusing and unintelligible. There were travelers from France and Italy, as well as England, waiting to board the ship that would take them to America. She was grateful for stewards that pointed them in the right direction.

The emigrants were awakened at 4:30 a.m. to board the ship. The *Ultonia* was due to leave the harbor with the tide. Aliisa had never seen a ship like the *Ultonia*. It was huge and had been previously used as a livestock carrier. She was directed to the cargo portion of the boat—the same place that had carried animals. The smell of cattle clung to the room that now had wide bunks built into the sides.

Third class, also called steerage, was tightly packed with emigrants. Aliisa stayed with the family she had met instead of bunking in the compartment for single women. They were served bread, water, soup, and small portions of sausage. The sanitary conditions were inadequate and the smell of human waste took away Aliisa's appetite. Aliisa could escape to the deck only during the hour allotted to third class passengers.

They had been at sea a couple of days when the young mother, Aliisa's companion, became wretchedly seasick. Her infant cried inconsolably. Aliisa held, rocked, and sang to the infant while the father tended to his wife and the other child. This kept Aliisa below deck for a couple of days, and as the ship rocked with the waves she battled nausea. Sound sleep was impossible with the clamor and closeness of so many other people. Sleep came in short intervals.

When the father was able to take the infant, Aliisa escaped to the deck of the ship. She drew in the fresh breaths of sea air, wanting to cleanse her body from the rank aura of the hold. She, along with other travelers, clung to the railing and looked with awe at the huge expanse of water. She fingered the letter of sponsorship from her brother and the description of her itinerary that was in her pocket. Her brother promised a better life in this place called Michigan. He said the mines were producing wealth. She was clinging to *his offer of hope and the joy of meeting her brother again. She was looking forward to a new lifestyle, away from the rural farm.*

A cook or a maid wouldn't have to clean the barn and plant crops that failed. She tried to imagine this place, Copper Island. Was it like the cities in England?

When the ship arrived in Boston, she struggled to stay with her Finnish companions as the mass of ragged and travel-weary people disembarked. They were required to show proof of sponsorship and travel arrangements to the customs official. As Aliisa dug the wrinkled documents from her pocket, she saw her friends being directed to a room for further inspection.

After her papers were checked, she couldn't find her friends and wondered if they were being detained. The young mother was weak and frail after her illness during the voyage. Overwhelmed and alone, Aliisa was directed to a horse-drawn wagon and driven to the railroad station.

An official looked at her papers and directed her to a train. She continued on her way as the strange and nonsensical sounds of the English language assaulted her ears. She sat down on the train in relief and exhaustion. Now she just needed to make the right train connections in New York and Chicago. The train in Chicago would take her the rest of the way to Calumet Township. Her sustenance was the crisp rye bread that she had packed in her bag when she left Finland.

Chapter 8

IT WASN'T OFTEN that Karin's phone rang. Most often the caller was Dylan Cutter.

"How's my favorite nurse?" He would begin the conversation with words that were soothing to Karin, and she was grateful to have someone to talk with. The calls were brief, but Karin was pleased that Dylan was interested in her.

She was surprised when Abigail called. Karin had microwaved a frozen meal for dinner and was just sitting down when the phone rang. The sound of Abigail's voice was pleasant. "How's it going? We've been waiting to hear from you, hoping you'll come for Thanksgiving."

"Oh, I know. Sorry. Can't decide if I want to do the long drive again."

"Well, I have a suggestion and a favor to ask. I have a friend at Michigan Tech who needs a ride down to Chicago the weekend before Thanksgiving, and I would like to do some shopping. Dr. Larson is giving me time off. If I drive down, would you be free to shop with me? I could stay with you Monday night, and Tuesday we could drive back," Abigail said.

"I'd love to shop with you! But I'll have to look at my work schedule. Can you hang on?" Karin reached for the calendar clipped to the refrigerator.

"We could shop on Monday, but I have to work on Tuesday."

"That's okay. We could drive on Wednesday. I can find things to do while you're at work."

"I'll have to find someone to cover a shift on the weekend. I'll find a way. Yes, come."

Abigail said that she would plan to be at Karin's apartment on Monday morning. Karin's mood lifted, and she spent the evening happily cleaning and organizing her apartment. She was looking forward to a girl's day out and then a holiday weekend.

On the Monday morning before Thanksgiving, Abigail appeared at Karin's apartment with an overnight bag in hand. Her hair was in the usual braid. She was wearing a pair of jeans and a white knit shirt.

Karin offered her coffee, and the two women sat down to plan their strategy for a day of shopping.

"What are you shopping for?" Karin asked.

"I'd like to find some casual slacks, running shoes, and a nice dress," Abigail said.

"Well, we could check out TJ Maxx, and maybe Kohl's or Lord & Taylor."

"I'd like to try Lord & Taylor," Abigail said.

"We could go Nordstrom Rack for shoes. We might want to stop by Rhonda's Resale. Every now and then I find something there."

"I'm glad I'm shopping with you. Let's go."

Abigail found some slacks at TJ Maxx. Both women found shoes at Nordstrom Rack. All the walking made them hungry, and they stopped for lunch at Panera.

After lunch, they went on to Lord & Taylor and sorted through the dress racks. Karin held up one dress after another. Finally Abigail took three dresses to the dressing room.

Karin critiqued each dress, and after much discussion, they decided that none of them were what Abigail had in mind.

"Are you up for one more shop? We could stop by Rhonda's Resale."

"Okay. I guess so."

Abigail entered the shop timidly. Karin led her to a rack of dresses and began rifling through the rack. She selected two dresses. One was A-line, black and gray woven fabric with a white collar. The other was a skirt and jacket in a rich jade green.

"Is there a place to try these on?" Abigail said.

Karin led Abigail to the dressing room, which was a partitioned space with a curtain. Abigail glanced around noticing other customers. Karin noticed her hesitation and she said, "Don't worry. I'll stand guard."

Abigail tried the black and gray dress first. Karin cocked her head, "Hmm . . . no."

Abigail tried the green suit and Karin nodded her approval. "With your hair down and gold earrings . . . very fine."

They spent a little more time looking and Karin found a blue sweater. They brought their selections to the clerk and were delighted with the price paid.

"I need to go shopping with you more often," Abigail said.

During the drive to Upper Michigan, Abigail and Karin had plenty of time to talk. Karin asked Abigail how her patients managed to get through labor without an epidural.

"It's important that my patients are free to move about and change position. I monitor them intermittently and allow them to walk, sit in a rocking chair, or use the birthing ball. They are able to listen to their body and respond."

"But they have pain," Karin said. "How do you manage that?"

"The pain is actually instructive. It encourages women to move to advantageous positions. It also gives me information. Sometimes I will assist with massage. Or I will suggest warm compresses or cold packs."

"But some of your patients get epidurals, don't they?"

"If labor is progressing slowly and a woman is exhausted, yes. At that point I call Dr. Larson in."

Eventually Abigail brought up the subject of Karin's roommate.

"Lori's death has been pretty hard for you," Abigail said.

"I'm doing okay," Karin said. She didn't want to appear weak to Abigail. Even though she had spilled her emotions with Dylan, now she kept her emotions tightly wrapped inside.

"Karin, I can see the pain in your eyes," Abigail said. "It's okay to talk about it." Abigail waited.

"It's complicated," Karin said. "Lori was a good person. She had a boyfriend and was full of life and fun." Karin paused and then continued, "I recently discovered that she took the abortion pill, and it may have caused her death."

"Oh, no, that's awful!" Abigail said and then became silent while she processed the information. What could she say? Life was precious. She had fought so hard for life in Africa. To take pills to destroy life and then die from it . . . what could she say?

Finally Abigail broke the silence, "Where did she get the pills?"

"I don't know, but I believe that it was an abortion clinic," Karin said. "I think that she had problems and called the clinic on the phone, and they gave her the prescription for pain medication without seeing her. I tried to find out which clinic and the doctor whose name is on the pill container, but haven't been able to."

An inner voice was cautioning Abigail to listen, but instead she said, "I don't understand why anyone would have casual sex, get pregnant, and then try to fix the situation by taking a pill."

Karin's face heated up. "It wasn't casual sex. Lori had been dating Mike for a year. Mike broke up with Lori when she became pregnant.

What was she supposed to do? She grew up without a father—do you think she wanted to raise a child without a father?"

"I'm sorry," Abigail said. She tried to change the subject but Karin shut down. The subject was too painful. There was silence in the car for some time until Abigail put on a CD of classical music.

Thanksgiving dinner was held at the Keskitalo home. Karin and Abigail arrived with the Aaltio family at noon. The scent of roasting turkey and freshly baked rolls teased their appetite. The women joined Helen and Mary in the kitchen. Helen gave directions for a few final preparations.

Karin took it all in with a bit of awe. Including herself there were five women scurrying in and around the kitchen. Helen was wearing a colorful bib apron and was directing the activity. She asked Rita to taste the potatoes and add more salt if needed. Karin noticed a vegetable dish that she didn't recognize, and Mary explained that it was a rutabaga casserole.

Some of the men and boys were watching football on TV. A couple of them had gone to pick up Aunt Lily. She lived in an assisted living facility but joined them on holidays.

Karin watched with fascination when Helen pulled the turkey out of the oven. It was a twenty-pound turkey covered with a white, butter-saturated cloth. As she lifted the cloth, the perfectly browned turkey was unveiled. Helen noticed Karin's interest.

"I soak a piece of cotton or muslin in butter and lay it over the turkey. It browns perfectly that way," she explained. Helen wiggled the turkey leg, "See how easily this moves? That's how you know the turkey is done."

After letting the turkey rest for fifteen minutes, Helen began to scoop out the cornbread dressing from the cavity. The aroma of turkey, onions, and sage spread through the kitchen. As she called her husband into the kitchen to carve the turkey, she heard the front door opening. "Here's Aunt Lily now."

Karin saw an elderly woman walking toward the kitchen. She held herself erect with the aid of a cane. Her hair was snowy white and had the look of a permanent that was wearing out. Her head was covered with loose curls and a little frizz. She glanced around the room and her eyes fixed on Karin. She studied her for a moment.

"*Oletko Soumalainen?*"

Mary whispered to Karin, "She asked if you are Finnish."

"My grandmother was Finnish," Karin said.

Mary stepped over to Aunt Lily, "I'd like you to meet my friend, Karin." As Karin smiled and extended her hand Mary continued, "Karin, this is my great-aunt, Lily. She has lived in this area all her life."

"*Hauska tavata,*" Aunt Lily said.

"Aunt Lily, Karin doesn't speak Finnish," Mary said gently.

Aunt Lily feigned a shocked look, wondering how a person could be Finnish and not understand Finnish. "Okay." She looked around the kitchen. "Where should I sit?"

Mary was released to entertain Aunt Lily. Abigail and Karin were commissioned to set the table. The overcrowded kitchen began to clear.

At last it was time to eat, and Helen called everyone to the table. When they all sat down, there were thirteen around the dining room table: Helen and Matt Keskitalo; their son, Jim, and his wife, Lynne; Mary and Jason; great Aunt Lily; Rita and John Aaltio; their sons, Paul and Ray; Abigail and Karin.

Matt Keskitalo offered a prayer of thanksgiving. Helen read a psalm from the Bible. And then there was a joyful passing of many dishes. Karin was drinking in the experience. Thanksgiving dinners with her Dad had been quiet affairs. Usually her Grandmother Lindale had ordered a prepared meal from the local grocery store, or they had gone out to eat.

As they ate, Rita mentioned a kantele concert that was going to be held at the Finnish American Heritage Center in a couple of weeks. "It's too bad you can't be here for that, Karin," Mr. Aaltio said. Mr. Aaltio never let an opportunity to reflect on Finnish culture go by. He was an educator who delighted in his Finnish roots.

"What's a kantele?" Karin said.

John Aaltio sat up in his chair, and motioning with his hands, explained the kantele. "It is an ancient Finnish instrument, a stringed instrument. Usually has five strings. It's angular in shape and is held in the lap when played. The rune singers accompanied themselves with the kantele."

"And what's a rune singer, Dad?" Abigail asked for Karin's benefit.

"Someone who recited poetry stories set to rhythm. Remember, before books were available, stories were passed along through oral tradition."

The references to ancient Finland and tradition were like a wind that stirred Karin's spirit. Like fall leaves carried on a gentle breeze, reminders of her Finnish heritage flitted around the dinner table.

Conversation at the table continued. "Do you have your Christmas cards done, Rita? You are always first, getting your cards out." Helen said.

With the mention of Christmas cards, Karin remembered the postcards and letter that she had brought with her. "After dinner could I show you some postcards and a letter that I found in my grandmother's things? They are all in Finnish. Maybe someone could translate them for me."

"Sure, I'd be glad to translate," Rita said.

"Can I pass anything to anyone?" Helen said as she looked around the table. The menfolk groaned with contentment. There was plenty of food left.

"I couldn't eat another bite," Matt said. "A wonderful meal, Helen."

"While the young ones clear up, I'll lay down," Aunt Lily said. Mary led Aunt Lily to the guest room and helped her lay down. She offered her an afghan and helped her cover her legs. "Make sure you get me for dessert."

After dishes had been washed and put away, Karin had the opportunity to bring out the antique mail. She sat down next to Rita and showed her the postcards. "My grandmother grew up on a farm near Calumet and she kept these. They might have been her mother's."

Rita smiled and said, "How pretty! These are so quaint."

"Do you know what it says?" Karin asked.

Rita turned the card over and translated the words.

"Dear Aliisa, How are you? I'm planning to come to Calumet with my brother on the weekend. I want to know about your job. I hope to meet you on Sunday.
Your friend always, Hanna."

"I guess I was kind of surprised to see postcards dating from about 1905," Karin said.

"This community was booming economically in the early 1900s" John said. "And then the miner's strike took place, and after World War I the mines went into a gradual decline."

"Some of the Finnish miners went back to a lifestyle that they knew, subsistence farming," Matt said.

"What's a subsistence farm?" Karin asked.

"Usually the family kept a couple of cows, some chickens, and raised a garden. They produced everything that they needed to survive and earned a little money selling milk and eggs."

"We could drive out to the Hanka Homestead tomorrow," Mary suggested. "It's an example of a subsistence farm."

Jason's eyebrows went up. "Are you sure? It's not the best time of year to drive out there."

"It's one of the sites in the National Historic Park now. It should be easier to get to. There is a nice cafe on the way. We could have lunch out, stop by my favorite shop, and then see the homestead."

"Lynne and I would love to go with you, but we have another commitment. Peter might want to go with you. He's always looking for an opportunity to explore the wilderness," Jim said.

"Wilderness?" Karin said.

"It's woods and farmland. The roads are a little sparse—some are gravel," Mary explained.

"I have office hours tomorrow, so I can't go. But I'll have dinner with you," Abigail said. Evelyn Larson had invited Abigail, Karin, Mary, and Jason for dinner. She had no children of her own and found pleasure in entertaining young adults.

The postcards were passed around the room. There was some chuckling over the pictures and sentiments expressed on the face of the postcards. Abigail read one out loud, "Love me and the world is mine."

Mary picked up one with a Christmas scene and read: "Thoughts of a friend at Christmas time, hold echoes sweet as a silver chime. And spread a glow so warm and clear, the season yields no brighter cheer."

Rita held the Finnish letter and looked it over. "It will take me a while to translate this. I'll need to decipher the handwriting." As she said this, the group heard a muffled cry.

"Help, oh, please help me!"

Mary jumped up and ran to the guest room. Aunt Lily had gotten herself tangled in the afghan. It was wrapped around her legs and she was struggling to sit up. Helen had followed Mary into the room, and together they unwound the afghan from her legs and helped her up.

They led her out to an easy chair. Helen said, "Well, I think it's time we served dessert. I'll put the coffee on."

Rita put the Finnish letter down on a lamp table and got up to help Helen. Karin put away the postcards but forgot the letter.

Chapter 9

The first class mail includes 3,000 sealed letters and about 600 postal cards. The second-class mail is composed entirely of newspapers. Third class mail is made up of printed matter, circulars, and photographs, and reached the very credible total daily of 1,500.

—*Calumet News*, October 19, 1907

WHEN ALIISA ENTERED the boarding house, she was pleased to find a postcard from Hanna. All of the boarders were Finnish, and it was a welcome relief to come home to her own people after working in the house of a wealthy store owner. She had learned the routines for washing clothes and house cleaning but was limited in communication. It was mentally tiring to spend the day among English speaking people. As she looked at the postcard, she was refreshed by words in her own language.

She was beginning to make friends at the Finnish Lutheran Church. Every nationality had their own church in the mining town, giving immigrants an opportunity for friendship and connection in America. There was a church on almost every corner in Calumet.

The churches provided community for the influx of people that had left their homeland. After the Sunday evening meeting at the Finnish church, the women served coffee by turns. It was pleasant to relax with a cup of coffee and a piece of cake. Aliisa had met Hanna at one of these meetings.

Aliisa and Hanna discussed their jobs and the houses they worked in. The houses were bigger and fancier than any they had seen in Finland. Bankers and merchants were reeling in profits from mine share speculation.

Captain Hoatson, a Scotsman, had made a fortune through the Calumet and Arizona Mining Company. The newspaper said that he was building a palatial mansion in Laurium. Aliisa and Hanna shared pieces of gossip about the mansion. The cedar columns and a porcelain-tiled porch were visible from the street. Some of the windows were brightly colored stained glass. People whispered about the icebox accessible from the street and the murals painted on the walls by hired artists. It was opulence that miners could not comprehend.

Aliisa and Hanna both dreamed of having their own homes. They had new ideas after working in nicely furnished houses. Perhaps they would have wallpaper and a fine dining room. The Finnish women had dreams but found it difficult to advance in the mining town. They earned just enough to provide for themselves.

The Calumet Finnish Ladies Society held meetings. One of the goals was to assist Finnish women with education and independence. This group produced a newspaper called the Naisten-Lehti. They also developed a lending library of 400 books and ten different Finnish and American newspapers and magazines.

Aliisa and the other women at the boarding house passed around the current edition of the Naisten-Lehti. The paper was a source of encouragement for Aliisa and also kept her abreast of women's issues in her homeland.

Finnish had little similarity with any of the other languages spoken in Calumet, and because Finnish had just thirteen consonants, many phonetic sounds in English and other tongues were unrecognized by the Finnish ear. If Aliisa had been exposed to English as a child, she would have learned to identify the sounds that slipped past her ear.

The Finnish speaking population was an island among the many nationalities. Aliisa was hoping to find time to attend some of the English *classes organized by the Calumet Finnish Ladies Society. Learning English was a long and tedious project for the Finns. Many adult Finnish immigrants never learned English. Aliisa hoped to have the time and energy.*

The weekends were filled with social activities. The upper class attended events at the Calumet Theater. Concerts, plays, and famous people appeared on stage, and the theater was full to overflowing. Just down the road from the theater, the Michigan House was a popular saloon. In a couple of years, it would be taken over by the Bosch Brewing Company. This company had plans for an ornate bar, a buffet, and a smoking lounge for gentlemen only.

The immigrant miners and maids found cheaper entertainment. On some Saturdays, Aliisa and her brother and a couple of others from the boarding house rode the trolley to Electric Park, located at the end of the trolley line. They brought along a picnic supper and stayed for the evening.

A huge Electric Park sign, made up of hundreds of light bulbs, lit up the park. Additional lights were strung around the perimeter. The Calumet & Hecla orchestra played for those who wished to dance. It was an opportunity to meet other men and women. On one particular weekend, her brother's coworker from the mines came along with them. Jan had been in the United States for a couple of years. Jan and Matti were both trammers in the Wolverine mine.

Chapter 10

HEN MARY AND Jason picked up Karin on Friday morning, Peter was with them. He came with his camera around his neck. He smiled at Karin and said, "So you are going to see a few of our attractions. It's a different arena compared to the city."

The four young people headed out to Chassell. They stopped at a shop that highlighted nature art. Photographs of waterfalls, the coastline of Lake Superior, wild animals, and birds adorned the walls. Calendars that focused on wildflowers, birds, and butterflies were displayed on racks.

A friendly and vivacious woman greeted them. Her brown hair, streaked with gray, was twisted into place with a comb. She had dangling earrings and a beaded bracelet.

"Ah, Peter, welcome! Perhaps you have more photographs?"

Peter smiled. "Have my photos been selling?"

"I have just one left. The photographs taken in Estivant Pines are all gone."

"What is Estivant Pines?" Karin asked.

"It's a forest of magnificent trees near Copper Harbor," Peter replied.

"Could I see the one photograph that you have left?" Karin asked.

The manager sorted through a group of photos and pulled out one. It was a picture of an eagle soaring over a still lake.

"Are there eagles around here?" Karin asked.

"Yeah. There's a growing population. There's a visible nest along Portage Lake," Peter replied.

Glass birds, polished stones, and driftwood were set out with scented candles and ceramic giftware. Bookshelves were filled with books on local history and wildlife, as well as cookbooks.

Peter picked up a pamphlet about the Hanka Homestead and showed it to Karin. The booklet had pictures of the original settlers and a map showing the location of the homestead in relation to a small inland lake, Otter Lake. He turned the pages to find a diagram of the inside of the house.

"We won't be able to go in the house now. During the summer the house and buildings are open. But here you can get an idea of the inside." The diagram showed a small kitchen-pantry-work area that opened to a square room that served as a living area and bedroom. The second floor was a bedroom.

While Peter and Karin explored the shop together, Mary picked out a few cards and browsed through the books and ceramics. The woodsy scent and the assortment of nature scenes were invigorating.

As they left, Peter promised to bring in more photographs. Karin was thoughtful as they walked out to the car. Peter was unassuming about his talent as a photographer. Their next stop was going to be the cafe.

The little restaurant was plain but neat and clean. The aroma of coffee and fresh baked rolls was welcoming. Booths lined one wall, and formica tables and chairs filled the open space. They seated themselves and a teenage waitress brought menus. She greeted them with a shy smile and mentioned that the soup of the day was turkey vegetable.

"Sounds great to me," Karin said. "Even though we just had turkey yesterday, I'll have the soup." Karin was enjoying the day, soaking in the comfort of companionship. The small town atmosphere was a huge change from Chicago, and she was enjoying it. The pace was slow. The four young people ordered their lunch and talked about Mary and Jason's plans for the coming year. When their food came, they ate leisurely. A couple of times someone paused at their table, and Mary introduced a family friend.

The drive out to the Hanka Homestead took them down a narrow gravel road and through forested land. Pine and cedar trees mingled with the barren deciduous trees. "This is pretty remote," Karin commented.

Jason was at the wheel and turned to Peter. "Let me know when we are close. I've been here once before but can't remember exactly where the homestead is." A serene lake surrounded by dark green pine trees and the snow-sprinkled branches of leafless trees came into view.

"That's Otter Lake," Peter said. "I think we missed a turn. Let's go back."

"There are no road signs. How do you know where to go?" Karin asked.

"No problem," Jason said. "We'll find it."

He turned the car around and drove back to a T in the road where they had turned right. The path to the left was narrow and rutted. Melted snow left muddy patches. Mary said, "I don't think we want to try that path." Jason stopped the car pondering which way to go.

"Just a minute," Peter said as he jumped out of the car and walked over to the edge of the narrow road, and peered into the trees. He came back with an announcement. "That blue sign says Hanka and points down the rutted path."

Jason shrugged and started down the path. The car lurched over potholes and Mary said, "I don't think we should be driving here." She had just finished her statement when a log across the road prevented them from driving any further.

"Now what?" Jason said.

"We can walk the rest of the way," Peter responded.

Karin and Mary looked dubious. "Come on," said Peter. "It's a little hike, but it's doable."

The group got out of the car and followed Peter down the lane. It seemed like they had walked a mile when they came to a sign at the homestead driveway. The driveway itself was long, and only after ten minutes of walking did they come to a gate and a sign commemorating the homestead as a Keweenaw National Historic Site. In the distance they could see log buildings.

"The house is over there on the hillside," Mary said, pointing.

"Oh, we can get closer. Come on," Peter said as he climbed over the gate.

Mary started to protest, but Jason climbed over and Karin followed. "Put your foot here," Peter instructed as he gave Karin a hand.

Reluctantly, Mary grasped the gate and struggled for footing. Jason leaned over the gate, pulling her up and over. They followed the drive as it wound through the property. Peter pointed out the barn, the sauna, and a deteriorating chicken coop. They walked up to the house, and Jason pointed to the orchard behind it. "They had quite a few apple trees."

"Some of those trees are heirloom varieties," Peter said. "I've read that the immigrants brought seeds from the old country for their gardens."

"I can't believe someone lived out here. It is so remote," Karin commented. "It's amazing they survived the winter."

"The old Finns were great pioneers," Mary said. "My great, great-grandfather built log cabins and barns like this."

They walked around the hilly site, sometimes slipping on a patch of soft snow. Peter pointed out the various buildings; the barn with a portal for horses to pull up and unload hay, the pigpen, the outhouse, the blacksmith building, the milk house, the sauna, and the root cellar. As they surveyed the site, Karin tried to imagine a family working this farm. It seemed lonely.

As they walked back down the driveway, they caught a glimpse of a porcupine disappearing into the underbrush. "He must be heading back to his den. Don't often see a porcupine in daylight," Peter said.

Mary started to sing softly, "*Piikkisika, piikkisika, porrkenpain,* that's the song they sing among the northern pine . . ."

Jason turned to Mary, his eyes crinkled with amusement. "What are you singing?"

"It's a little song about the porcupine. My grandmother used to sing it when we took walks."

"Shhh," Peter said, putting a finger to his lips. The little group stood still and silent. They heard a resounding *tap, tap, tap* occurring in rapid rhythm. It was the sound of a woodpecker echoing through the woods. They craned their necks trying to locate him. Peter had his camera out, hoping to get a picture.

They turned out onto the rutted lane. They were carefully choosing their steps when a deer came crashing out of the woods, fifty yards ahead of them, and crossed the lane. Seconds later, a large gray animal appeared, leaping and strong in his pursuit of prey. Peter snapped pictures in quick succession.

"I think that was a wolf," Jason said, frozen to the spot.

As they stood together silent for several minutes, they strained their ears to hear the snap of branches. They heard a thump. Did the wolf get his prey?

"If there was one wolf, are there more?" Karin asked.

"I think we should get back to the car," Mary said. Mary and Karin walked quickly toward the car. Karin's foot slipped on a rut and she went down, twisting her ankle. Mary came alongside and helped her up. Karin winced when she took a step. Mary offered her arm, and Karin clutched it for support as she made her way to the car.

When they got to the car, neither Jason nor Peter were in sight. The women stood outside the car—it was locked and Jason had the keys. "Where did they go?" Mary asked. "Jason," she yelled.

Chapter 11

A parade in which hundreds of strikers participated, and headed by "Mother Jones" was formed at union headquarters, and proceeded direct to the Palestra . . . "We demand an eight-hour day and a minimum wage schedule. . . . Richest mines but poorest miners."

—*Calumet News*, August 6, 1913

ALIISA SAT ACROSS the table from Jan while the baby slept in the cradle. Jan's work clothes gave testament to the dirt and grime of the mines. His hands were bruised and scratched. Although he had washed his face and hands when he came home, a residue of gray remained. Rough stubble covered his cheeks and chin. Aliisa was fidgeting with a button on the sleeve of her dress. They spoke in Finnish to each other. The two oldest children, both boys, had gone to bed.

"Saima came by today. She said that Waino passed away—his injuries were too severe and the doctor couldn't save him," Aliisa said. "A group of us will make meals for his family and do what we can, but it is going to be very hard for them in the coming year."

Jan shook his head. "How many is it? At least ten miners we know have died this year. I dread going down those deep shafts, and it seems that I rarely see sunlight anymore."

"Have there been any improvements in the mines since the strike was settled?"

"They made a few changes, but it is still dangerous. We are paid a pittance when you consider how much wealth the mines are pulling in," Jan said bitterly.

"Can't you get a better position? You would be good as a supervisor, and you could push for the changes that you know need to be made," Aliisa said.

"You know how they don't like Finns. . . . we talk funny and wear homemade clothes. . . . they think we are stupid." Jan's fingers tightened in a fist. "We have jobs because we are willing to do what no one else wants to do—some of the lazy guys have warned me to slack off. They are afraid of being asked to work harder."

Jan reached out for Aliisa's hand. "I'm thinking seriously about Paul's offer. He will sell us forty acres from his homestead. He can't farm 120 acres. We can have our own land, develop our farm, and take care of ourselves."

Aliisa looked down, tears in her eyes. "It's going to be just like Finland. I know how much work a small farm is. I like living in town." She shuddered inwardly with the memories of barely surviving on the farm in Finland. She had come here to have a different life.

"Aliisa, you have to think about this. I don't want to work in the mines forever, not even for another year. In Finland we didn't have the opportunity to own a farm. It is different here. It will be our land, our farm," Jan said, and his face was alight with hope.

"Hanna and Jouko purchased the homestead adjoining Paul's land. We won't be in town, but we will have neighbors."

Aliisa said, "I don't want to be miles from town." She wanted to say more, but she understood how difficult and dangerous the mine work was for Jan. She did not want him to take up logging either. Her brother Matti was working for a logging camp, away for long stretches of time. She wanted to stay in town. The trolley cars made it easy to visit friends and shop. The mining company supported good schools. The Calumet Library was a beautiful building and carried Finnish books and newspapers. Her dream was to have a house in town.

Jan's love for Aliisa had helped him stay with the mining job, but now he saw an opportunity to provide for his family in a different way. He knew that subsistence farming was hard, but it would allow him to be his own man.

Tears streaked Aliisa's cheeks. Jan paced, not knowing what to say. Aliisa's hopes and desires were vivid ideals, but concern for her husband tugged at her heart. She did not know how to resolve the conflict in her mind. For a couple of days they barely spoke to each other. The lack of harmony was a heavy weight.

One night Jan asked Aliisa to pray with him. Jan's patience and his prayer allowed Aliisa to resolve the struggle in her heart. She loved and respected her husband. She said, "I will help you build a farm."

Jan kissed Aliisa tenderly. Her respect for him was a tonic; her body was a comfort. Some men resorted to alcohol but Jan was committed to his wife and family.

A year later, Jan purchased the forty acres of land. Friends and neighbors helped build a log home on the forested land fifteen miles from town. The family began the long and difficult task of carving a farm out of the woods. They cut down trees and removed the stumps. The word about town was that only the Finlanders were foolish enough and stubborn enough to clear the land for farming.

They had sisu, Finnish inner strength and determination. They were resourceful and accomplished in woodsmen skills. They collaborated with friends. When the land was cleared, they planned their crops around a short growing season.

Chapter 12

FIFTEEN MINUTES LATER, Jason and Peter returned to the car. "Where did you go, Mary?" asked Jason.

"Where did we go? Where did you go?"

"We followed the trail of the wolf a little way into the woods. I thought you were with us. Peter wanted to get another picture."

Mary rolled her eyes. "Sure, like we were going to run into the woods. We started toward the car, and Karin turned her ankle. We've been waiting for you in the cold."

Peter was checking the photos on his digital camera and missed the conversation. "I got a couple of good shots," he said.

Jason opened the car door, "I'm sorry Karin. Let's get you inside."

The ride back to Mine Harbor was quiet. Peter's enthusiasm for his pictures didn't extend to Karin or Mary. Karin was cold, and her ankle ached. Mary was annoyed with Jason for setting off with Peter. They rode in silence and dropped off Peter at his car as he had other plans for the evening.

Karin, Mary, and Jason arrived at the Larson's house with dampened spirits. Evelyn's warm welcome put Karin at ease. Mary explained that Karin had turned her ankle.

"You probably should ice it," Evelyn said. She pointed to the easy chair. "Sit down. I'll be right back."

She returned with an ice pack, pulled a footstool over for Karin, and encouraged everyone to sit down. Evelyn's pleasure in having the young people in her home shone through her smile.

When Evelyn learned that Karin was a nurse, she quickly recognized an opportunity to recruit for Harbor Hospital. "We need experienced nurses. Have you ever considered moving to a small town?"

"Well, actually no," Karin said. She wondered what it would be like.

"Mary, make sure you explain the advantages of our community to Karin," Evelyn said. Mary nodded and tried to hide her amusement. Evelyn knew that Chicago had museums, cultural events, and restaurants. Mine Harbor was a hard sell by comparison.

Abigail arrived and Evelyn offered everyone mulled cider. Abigail explained that Dr. Larson was finishing up at the hospital but expected to be home in a half hour. They decided to wait for him, and Abigail picked up a book from the coffee table. "Are you familiar with the *Kalevala?*" she asked Karin.

Karin shook her head.

Abigail explained, "It's a Finnish epic. Dad says that it stirred national pride in Finland. He teaches a class about it." Abigail had grown up with parents who steered her to a love of books. She had a natural inclination to share literature. She continued on trying to capture Karin's interest. "It's a collection of ancient poetry, part of an oral tradition. Singers recited the poems, and in the 1800s the poems were transcribed."

Mary added, "It has epic heroes—one named Vainamoinen—but stories of creation and the Virgin Mary are mixed in also."

"Really?" Karin said.

Abigail explained, "When people in the villages didn't have books, stories were passed on through recitation. The rhythmic poetry helped the singer recite the story. It's hard to think about what it was like before the printing press was invented."

Karin picked up the book. "Show me a poem about the Virgin Mary."

Mary thumbed through the book, then handed the open volume to Karin. Karin scanned the page. "Oh my gosh, Mary is in labor, running from place to place for shelter . . . and she gives birth in a stable where the animals provide sauna heat!" Karin began to read the lines out loud.

> *She stepped, tripped along*
> *To the room in the fir-clump*
> *To the stable on Tapo Hill.*
> *She said in these words:*
> *"Now breathe, my good horse*
> *over my troubled belly*
> *let some bath-steam loose*
> *send some bath-house warmth*
> *over my troubled belly*
> *where a wretch can be cared for*
> *one in trouble can be helped."*
> *And the good horse breathed*
> *let some bath-steam loose*
> *Sent some bath-house warmth*
> *Over her troubled belly.*
> *On Christmas Day God was born*
> *The best boy when it was cold*
> *Born upon a horse's hay*
> *At a straight-hair's manger-end.*

Karin laughed and said, "Wow, that's a different version."

Evelyn smiled. "I think the singers were conveying the story of Mary based on their own culture and experience. The recitation of these poems was entertainment and a way to remember significant events."

Dr. Larson arrived and the group moved to the dining room for dinner. Evelyn served meatballs in rich gravy with noodles, glazed carrots, and green beans. She set out a loaf of Swedish limpa bread.

There was a lively discussion of the Hanka homestead and other sites in the Keweenaw National Historical Park. Then Abigail shifted the conversation. "Dr. Larson, what do you know about the abortion pill?"

Karin gave Abigail a frigid look. Why was she bringing this up?

Abigail did not notice and went on. "Karin's roommate died suddenly a couple months ago. Karin thinks the abortion pill contributed to her death."

"Are you serious?" Mary said and looked to Karin. Karin didn't say anything and Mary continued, "I've heard about the morning after pill. Is that what you're talking about?"

Dr. Larson glanced from Abigail to Karin. "What did she take? The morning after pill is a heavy dose of hormones that aborts pregnancy before implantation. The abortion pill is a two-part medication that causes the uterus to abort a pregnancy that is further along."

Abigail looked toward Karin. "Tell him."

Karin told him about finding the empty container, labeled misoprostol, and gave a brief description of her observations when she arrived home from Florida.

"Misoprostol is the second medication—second part of the abortion pill. It's cheap and it does a great job causing the uterus to contract after childbirth. It is dangerous during pregnancy. It is used for abortion only if a woman is less than seven weeks beyond her last menstrual period. Do you know how far along Lori was in her pregnancy?"

"I didn't know that she was pregnant," Karin said. "But looking back, it's possible that she was."

"What was the cause of death?" Dr. Larson said.

"Septicemia was listed on the death certificate, but the hospital didn't know she had taken these pills." Karin replied. "Jenny and I tried to locate the doctor who prescribed the medications, but we weren't able to."

"What do you hope to accomplish by locating him? And if you find him, what do you think he is going to do about it?" Dr. Larson asked.

"What do you mean?" Karin was confused by this question.

"If the abortion pill caused her death, he doesn't want to know about it. He is not going to connect himself with this death if he can help it." Dr. Larson had practiced in a litigious climate. Malpractice claims had driven most doctors to a defensive posture.

Evelyn put a hand on her husband's arm. "If this drug is connected to a death, don't you think it should be reported? Is it possible that an abortion could lead to septicemia?"

"I know of a case where a woman developed septicemia after a miscarriage, but she survived. If any part of a dead fetus or placenta remains in the uterus it can become infected and cause pain. The uterus is a very blood rich center, especially with pregnancy. Infection can travel to the bloodstream and then to the whole body," Dr. Larson explained. He paused for a moment. "Was an autopsy done?"

Karin nodded.

"It would be helpful to know if the autopsy showed an enlarged uterus."

Mary saw that Karin was about to break down. She said, "I think we've discussed this enough."

Evelyn gazed compassionately at Karin, "I'm sorry about your friend. How is her family taking it?"

"Her mom is devastated. Lori was an only child raised by her mom. Her dad left when she was a little kid. He didn't even come to the funeral."

On impulse, Karin reached for her purse. She pulled out a pocket size album of photographs, removed a picture of Lori, and passed it around. A young woman with shoulder length auburn hair and a dimple in her cheek smiled as she flirted with the camera.

Dr. Larson studied the picture, trying to pinpoint what it was that captured his attention.

"So tragic, what a lovely young woman," Evelyn said. After an uncomfortable time of silence she spoke up, "I think it's time for dessert and coffee. I have some lemon cake."

She got up, and Mary followed her into the kitchen. Mary served coffee while Evelyn cut the cake. Karin hardly touched her dessert; she didn't feel like eating. She barely paid attention when the conversation turned to Mary and Jason's housing options in Indiana.

Evelyn commented, "We'll have the duplex available in January. Perhaps you would like to have a place in town, Abigail. And there is room for you to have a roommate."

After everyone left, Ben retired to his study. Lori's story brought to the surface his internal struggles. The line between health care and detrimental manipulation was fuzzy. The wonder of new discoveries overshadowed concerns. He recalled his enthusiasm for medical progress during college.

During one year of medical school he had been a naïve sperm donor. It was a way to earn extra cash, and a way to solve an infertility problem for an anonymous woman. He hadn't thought much more about it at the time. Years later he wondered if his donations had resulted in viable pregnancies for unknown women. Did he have biological children? Were they healthy and in good families?

Ben tried to avoid the enigmas within accepted medical practice, but tonight unwanted thoughts surfaced in his mind. The birth control pill, legalized under the right to privacy ruling, had been fairly new when he began his practice. It was heralded as the solution to unplanned pregnancy and provision of the pill became standard practice. But ten years later abortion was legalized. And now the abortion pill and the morning after pill were on the market.

During medical school the Hippocratic oath was described as: first of all, do no harm. The actual text of the oath, dating back to 400 BC, included a refusal to perform abortions, but a watered down version was popular when he was in medical school. It deleted all reference to abortion.

A friend and former colleague had recently joined a group of doctors affirming a restatement of the Hippocratic oath. He sent a copy of the oath, and Ben was startled when he read the text of the third paragraph.

> I will follow the method of treatment, which according to my ability and judgment, I consider for the benefit of my patient, and abstain from whatever is harmful or mischievous. I will neither prescribe nor administer a lethal dose of medicine to any patient even if asked nor counsel any such thing nor perform act or omission with direct intent deliberately to end a human life. I will maintain the utmost respect for every human life from fertilization to natural death and reject abortion that deliberately takes a unique human life.

He had never provided abortions, but he acknowledged the deeper issues in women's health care. After years of providing the pill, he saw the problems. He knew it manipulated a woman's delicate hormonal system, creating both risks and side effects. It altered the hormonal network in a woman's body. Sometimes a fertilized egg failed to implant in the uterine wall due to changes in the lining of the uterus.

Ben had looked at research studies indicating that women who used the pill for four years or more, prior to a full-term pregnancy, had increased risk of developing breast cancer. Instead of health promotion, the pill and its consequences were mischievous.

In addition, women often did not realize that as they aged, their fertility declined. Women couldn't always get pregnant when they wanted. As he kept pace with the treatments for infertility, he was aware of the ethical quandary.

Ben's group practice had performed in vitro fertilizations. The procedure led to questions about the extra embryos. What should be done? Keep them indefinitely or hand them over for research? Could the embryos be sold? Perhaps an infertile couple would want to buy a viable embryo. The dilemmas were piling up. Doctors could do so much with medication and technology, but should they?

Ben leaned back in his chair, tilting his head back. He had told his friend that he wanted to avoid the politics of health care and just practice medicine. Could he continue to retreat from these issues? He massaged the back of his neck and closed his eyes. Finally, he went up to the bedroom, hoping that Evelyn was asleep. She was in bed but still awake.

"Isn't there more you could do to help Karin?"

"What do you mean?" Ben asked.

"You still have contacts in Chicago. You can find out which clinic this Dr. Smith worked at." Evelyn said. "Something went wrong."

"And if I find out where this clinic is?"

"It's one more piece of information. Lori's mother might want to pursue legal action. Karin needs to do something to find resolution."

Ben looked at his wife with a mix of angst and tenderness. "I'll make a few phone calls." Ben sighed. "Could you call Karin and get all of the information on the pill container: date, the doctor's name, the prescription number, and pharmacy phone number?"

"I'll call tomorrow," Evelyn said.

"I can't promise anything, but I'll do my best." He couldn't change what had happened to Lori, but perhaps Evelyn had a point.

"Thank you, dear," Evelyn said. She put her arms around him and kissed him.

Karin and Abigail spent the night at Mary and Jason's. Their half of the duplex had the same restored woodwork as the Larson's place. Framed wedding photographs adorned the walls. The furniture was rustic, some of it secondhand.

Jason excused himself, and Mary led the women into the kitchen. She fixed a pot of tea and they settled themselves around the kitchen table. Mary noticed that Karin had withdrawn. "Are you okay, Karin?" she asked.

"I know you all think Lori was wrong to use the abortion pill. She didn't know it had the potential to kill her," Karin said.

"I think Dr. Larson is right. You should find out what the autopsy report showed," Abigail said. "Then you can decide if you should suggest legal action to Lori's mother. Please believe me, I'm sad about what happened to Lori."

"Someone should have told her about the risks. Someone should have insisted on checking her before giving her a prescription for pain medication." Karin could not keep her turbulent feelings inside. Mary came and put an arm around Karin.

"I am so sorry. Perhaps Mrs. Sander will pursue it." Mary wanted to lift the burden from Karin but didn't know how. Silently she prayed for Karin.

Abigail observed Karin with sympathy. "Mary, do you have anything like an ace bandage? I think we should wrap Karin's ankle." Mary rummaged around and found an old tee shirt that she cut to make a long strip of fabric. Abigail carefully wrapped Karin's ankle.

Karin thought about the choices Mary had made. "I guess you're glad that you waited until marriage for sex."

"I will tell you the truth. Sex has had its learning curve. Our first time was not what I expected. Jason and I are learning how to please each other. We want to give ourselves completely—it's getting better and better."

At that moment Jason entered the kitchen. "Well said, Mary," he said as he gathered her into his arms. He turned to Karin, "Don't give yourself to a man before the marriage vow, Karin."

Karin blushed. Abigail took in Jason and Mary's embrace and said, "I guess it's time for all of us to head off to bed." After quick goodnights,

Mary helped Karin pull out the sofa bed, and everyone settled in for the night.

Early in the morning Abigail was called to the hospital for a birth. Karin had breakfast with Mary and Jason, and they spent a leisurely morning together. After lunch, Abigail called and said she was heading home to catch a nap before the evening, when they would have their Saturday sauna.

Mary and Karin went out for a walk through town. Mary pointed out a weathered red stone building. "The stone in these old buildings was quarried from this area." After walking a few blocks they turned right. Mary pointed to a three-story brick building.

"There's Harbor Hospital—it's walking distance from the duplex."

Clouds had rolled in, and a fine misty sleet had started to fall. Karin shivered and Mary said, "It looks like we're in for a storm. I guess we should head back. Maybe we should get an early start driving to my aunt and uncle's place."

Karin looked forward to a typical sauna Saturday. Abigail said that there would be plenty of food, time for the sauna, and perhaps a few board games to boot. Karin wondered if Peter was planning to come and then pushed the thought away.

Chapter 13

In the rural areas the labor of the immigrant wife spelled the difference between success and failure. It took an American observer to see perhaps more clearly than husband and children the severity of her burden: "It was back-breaking, grubbing, lugging, tugging work with stumps and brush and roots that her body ached with weariness, sheer and utter. She bore numerous and close-timed children. She managed the slight family revenue. She had the responsibility of the little dairy."

She cooked and washed and sewed clothes; she tended the sauna . . .

—*The Finns in America*

*A*FTER FRIENDS AND *neighbors helped build their log cabin, Jan and Aliisa worked together to establish a home. The work was arduous and exhausting, but they tried to end each day with prayer. Their faith in God helped them to persevere.*

All of the family members took part in clearing the land. Tree stumps and brush had to be dug out to prepare fields for planting. They would plant potatoes, oats, and rye. Their survival depended on producing their own food. Jan hunted deer and fished, while Aliisa took charge of salting and smoking the game to preserve it.

Jan planned for the additional buildings: barn, outhouse, and chicken coop. He also had the task of securing clean water. He needed to procure income for the farm projects, so during the winter, Jan spent weeks at a time away at the logging camp.

When he had time, he built basic furniture to furnish their cabin and devised homemade tools for farming. Aliisa saved rags and extra pieces of cloth. Jan built a loom and Aliisa made rag rugs to cover the cold floors. She knitted socks and mittens, salvaged outgrown clothing, and sewed garments for her family. Jan and Aliisa were adroit in making a home.

Every Saturday the smoke sauna was heated. If Jan wasn't home, Aliisa built the fire and tended it during the day. Billows of smoke furled out of the vents. By evening the fire died down and the smoke cleared. The large heap of stones had absorbed heat all day and kept the sauna warm for baths. Everyone in the family was scrubbed clean and came out relaxed and ready for bed.

If Jan was home on Sunday mornings, he read from the Bible first. Then Aliisa brought out the aapinen for a lesson in Finnish. The aapinen contained pictures depicting words, and letter combinations demonstrating phonetic sounds. The two oldest children, Jeremy and Tim, were nine and seven years old. Six-year-old Lisa watched the babies.

Finnish families on neighboring farms held home church services on Sunday afternoons. Aliisa looked forward to one day of the week for socializing. At these meetings, a preacher led Bible teaching and the families found friendship and support. And of course coffee and pulla were always served. During the winter, travel to the Sunday meetings was an adventure. The family traveled on skis, pulling the little ones in a sled.

Aliisa and Jan and the neighbors in their Finnish community were committed to educating their children. They made plans for a school and hired the first teacher. The young man held classes in a log cabin. He had his hands full with a group of children, ages six to fourteen. He conducted classes in English, and taught reading, writing, and arithmetic. The older children attended sporadically because they were needed for chores at home.

One year, the children had a special Christmas program. They sang Christmas carols and memorized short poems in English. They also recited portions of the Kalevala in Finnish, as one of the adults strummed the kantele. Some of the folk poetry focused on the hero, Vainamoinen.

Aliisa was attentive to the recitation about the Virgin Mary, Marjatta. Mary's pregnancy and impending childbirth was depicted as difficult and fearful. The poetry dramatized Mary's search for a safe place to give birth.

As Aliisa listened to the poetry her thoughts turned to Finland. It was hard to be so far from family and traditions. In Finland they celebrated Christmas Eve by going to the cemetery, bringing evergreen wreaths and candles to decorate the graves of family members. The candles flickered with a brightness that shone in the long winter night. The sun barely skimmed the horizon during northern Finland's winter. Candlelight was a precious part of celebrating Jesus' birth. Jesus came into the world as the light of the world, bringing the hope of resurrection.

Then the family bathed in the sauna to prepare for the remaining festivities, including a Christmas Eve feast. She remembered the taste of butter-rich prune tarts and rice pudding enjoyed in the good years.

Early in the morning, while the sky was still dark, they went to church as a family. The church was decorated with evergreen branches and the glow of candles. These memories flitted through Aliisa's thoughts as she watched the children's Christmas program.

Aliisa was pregnant again, expecting her sixth child. She knew the difficulties of giving birth on an isolated farm. She had heard about Sofia Salmi. Sofia gave birth to her eighth child during the winter. Afterward she bled heavily, but the family couldn't get her to the hospital because of a snowstorm. Even with a sleigh they couldn't go the ten miles in the blinding snow, and Sofia died.

And it wasn't only giving birth that she was concerned about. She had struggled with this pregnancy, feeling overwhelmed with her responsibilities. She took care of the farm animals, cooked, cleaned, and instructed her children. Did she have the strength and energy to care for another baby?

During the summer months, days were set aside for berry picking. Aliisa knew where the wild blueberries grew. She packed a lunch, and the family spent the day filling pails with the little berries.

Aliisa had cultivated a patch of raspberry bushes in the garden and sent the children out to pick. She gradually stocked the shelves in the cellar with jars of canned berries, a flavorful addition to their diet and a source of nutrition.

Summer and fall, she had worked hard to store food for the winter months. The older children helped with the garden and the harvest, filling the root cellar with bags of potatoes, rutabagas, and apples.

Later that night Aliisa opened the family Bible, which illuminated the Virgin Mary's story. She was chosen by God to give birth to Jesus, but it was not easy. Required to make a trip when her pregnancy was at term, Mary trusted God. Her faith in God gave her courage. God provided for her and the safe birth of Jesus. Aliisa read the Bible account and prayed, confessing her own fears and asking for God's help.

She was due to give birth the last week of January and hoped that the midwife would arrive in time. Aliisa planned to have the sauna warmed, and when the labor pains came on hard, she would go there for the birth. Mary gave birth to Jesus in a stable under difficult circumstances. Like Mary, Aliisa would have to depend on God for help.

Chapter 14

IT WAS LATE afternoon when Mary, Jason, and Karin started out for the Aaltio's home. Misty sleet had changed to a heavy, wet snow mixed with rain. The car fishtailed slightly when Jason stopped at a stoplight.

The roads seemed to get more slippery as they went along. Jason gave his full attention to the road, and they inched along as he avoided quick stops. Mary and Karin chatted but kept looking out the window at the treacherous weather. They were relieved to arrive at their destination. Rita opened the door and hugged each of them.

"The sauna is warm. John and I will go first, and then you girls can go. The boys will be last. Paul, offer everyone something to drink," Rita said.

"Okey-dokey. What would you ladies like? Sparkling apple juice, iced tea, Coke . . . hot chocolate . . . coffee. I could check the fridge . . ."

"The apple juice sounds great," Mary said and Karin agreed.

"Coke for me," Jason said.

As they sipped their drinks, Paul asked about the roads. "What's it like out there?"

"It's getting nasty," Jason said. "The roads are icing over."

Abigail came downstairs, brushing wisps of hair from her face. Her clothes were rumpled, and she appeared a little drowsy.

"Looks like you had a good nap," Mary said.

"Oh, it was good. I was up until five this morning. Tricia Johnson gave birth to a beautiful girl, eight pounds and eight ounces. So, I'm guessing it's time for the sauna. I should collect our towels. Are mom and dad in the sauna now?" Abigail asked Paul.

Paul nodded, "Yeah. Ray is in the kitchen putting together his prize-winning chili."

"He won a prize with this recipe at the church fall festival," Abigail explained. "Well girls, I guess we should get our clean clothes and towels ready."

When Rita and John came out of the sauna, the women were all set for their turn. This was Karin's second sauna, and she relaxed in the penetrating steam. She stayed in longer than the first time but not as long as Abigail and Mary.

As the women stepped out of the sauna building, Mary slipped and just caught herself from falling. "It's icy out here," she cried. The sleet was still coming down, mixed with rain. They walked slowly, watching each step on the way back to the house.

When they entered, the aroma of fresh baked rolls greeted them. Rita had a turban around her damp hair and wore a cotton shirt and pants. She had stacked bowls on the counter next to a large pot of chili and was now slicing sausage and cheese.

"The sauna is free," Rita called out. "Are Jim and Lynne and Peter coming?"

"They said they might be running late," Jason responded.

"Well, you'd better get your sauna now so we can eat before it gets too late."

Rita turned to the girls, "Get a cold drink, and then you can help set out the food."

Abigail poured glasses of ice water and then sat down to braid her wet hair. Mary pulled her hair back in a ponytail. Karin's short hair was drying in dark curls.

When the men returned from the sauna, Rita began ladling chili into bowls and asked everyone to sit down at the table. The dinner conversation was lively. Ray got lots of compliments on the chili. The men and women had been refreshed by the sauna, and they enjoyed each other's company.

A list of games was discussed and narrowed down to Guesstures, Scrabble, and Trivial Pursuit. They had cleared the table when the doorbell rang. Paul went to the door, and Karin, expecting to see Peter, was disappointed. Jim and Lynne Keskitalo came in.

"Where is Peter?" Jason asked.

"He was working on a computer problem at Tech. I think he's still planning to come," Jim said. "I hope he makes it. The roads are slick and ice is glazing the trees. The sleet and rain are still coming down."

"Have you two eaten? How about a bowl of chili?" Rita suggested.

"Thanks. We've already had dinner, but we'd like to take a sauna," Lynne said.

"We were just discussing games. Maybe we could start with Guesstures, and when you are out of the sauna, we could split up the group with some playing Scrabble and some playing Trivial Pursuit," Abigail suggested.

They drew numbers and Rita, Jason, Paul, and Karin were on one team. John, Ray, Mary, and Abigail were on the other. Paul was selected to choose a card first. He said, "The category is a thing." The word was *train*. He thought for a moment and then began a charade for his team. He put his hands on an imaginary steering wheel and pushed the brake with his foot.

Karin guessed, "Stop sign?"

Paul shook his head. He pretended to get out of a car, walked forward, made his arms stiff and moved them down like a railroad crossing gate.

Jason suggested, "Policeman."

Paul shook his head. Ray and Mary were laughing. Paul pretended that he was the train, trying to demonstrate the chug-a-chug-a rhythm.

Ray shouted, "Energizer bunny!"

John elbowed Ray, "You're not supposed to guess."

The timer went off. Paul said, "The word was *train*." His team groaned.

It was Mary's turn to pick a card. She picked *amnesia*. As she was considering how to act it out, the lights in the house went out. "Oh dear," Rita exclaimed. John waited to see if the lights would come back on, and then got up, feeling his way to the den. He groped for a flashlight in the desk drawer. Then he found candles and matches and handed them to Rita. When she had lit them, he said, "I'm going to get our lantern."

He made his way to the basement and came back with a battery-powered lantern. Rita said, "Why don't we have dessert while we wait for the electricity to come back on."

John set the lantern on the dining room table. Abigail and Rita brought out plates, forks, and pie. Rita cut the pie, and Abigail poured coffee from a thermos.

As the group gathered around the table, the noise of the wind picked up, and they felt a draft come through the room. The furnace was powered by electricity, so the heat was off. Rita left for a few moments and returned with her arms full. She put a sweater on and announced to the group, "There are more sweaters here and also some afghans if anyone wants one."

Lynne and Jim entered the room, faces flushed from the steam in the sauna. "The sauna was toasty warm when we let the fire die down. Thank goodness we were drying off when the lights went out." Lynne said.

"I wonder how extensive the outage is," Jim said.

Rita encouraged them to help themselves to some dessert. Conversation continued with Ray asking Karin about Chicago. He had never been there but had heard about the museums. "Have you gone to the Aquarium?"

Karin shook her head.

"They have beluga whales—did you know that?"

Before Karin could reply there was a sharp knock on the front door. When John opened it, Peter was standing there, his face white and drained of color. "I need help. There's a woman that needs help. Hurry!"

John, Abigail, and Jim grabbed their jackets and followed Peter outside. The ground was icy and sleet was falling. They had to pick their way carefully along the driveway to Peter's car. Huddled in the back seat, a woman was moaning. The man sitting next to her was squeezing her hand.

"What happened?" Abigail asked.

The man said, "We were on our way to the hospital . . ."

The woman shivered and moaned again.

Peter said, "I found them walking along the road. A short distance down the road their car is in the ditch."

"Her water bag broke when we were walking," the man explained. The woman was wearing a loose-fitting winter coat. Abigail peered at the young woman. At first glance her pregnancy was not apparent.

"Is she in labor?" Abigail exclaimed.

"Yes, we were on our way to the hospital . . ."

Paul joined the group outside. As the men realized the nature of the problem, they were wordless and just stood there.

Abigail knelt down to make eye contact with the woman. "Do you feel like you have to bear down?"

The young woman was bent over groaning. As the contraction subsided, she lifted her head. "No . . . I'm shaking . . . the contractions are strong," she said.

"Oh, my, we need to get her inside." Abigail looked to the men. "Help me get her inside. I can check her and see if we have time to get to the hospital."

The husband encouraged her to slide to the edge of the seat. He supported her back while John and Jim each took an arm and helped her stand.

"I can't walk," she whispered.

"Yes, you can," Abigail said firmly. The woman shivered again.

"I think we should go to the sauna," John Aaltio said. "The house doesn't have heat right now. Paul, go stoke the fire in the sauna stove."

Abigail turned to Jim, "Would you ask my mother to get blankets and as many towels as she can find? Have her bring them to the sauna."

John and the husband supported the woman, a hand on each arm. Abigail encouraged her to take one little step at a time. They were halfway to the sauna when she said, "I can't go any further."

The two men picked her up, their hands clasped to form support like a seat.

As they walked to the sauna, Abigail hurried ahead, stepping carefully. Jim, Rita and Karin were coming with the supplies she had asked for. Paul had hung the lantern on the shower rack. The door between the sauna and the shower room was open, and Paul was putting a couple chunks of wood in the stove. The fire crackled, and a glow of light and heat flowed out into the shower area.

"We are going to set up in a corner of the shower. Put blankets down there," Abigail said. "Then put a couple towels on the blankets. Place the rest of the towels on the sauna bench."

As Paul left, he held the door open for the men carrying the laboring woman. Her legs were shaking. Abigail and Karin helped the men ease her down on the towels and blankets.

Abigail asked the husband to help her undress his wife. John stepped outside. Karin stood by ready to help, but she was unnerved. They had no intravenous fluids, no medications, no fetal monitor, and no delivery room set-up.

Abigail explained to the young woman that she was a midwife. "I'd like to examine you, so we know how close you are to giving birth."

The young woman nodded and Abigail examined her. Abigail's facial expression changed to a frown. "It's breech," she said.

"Are you sure?" Karin asked, thinking of the impossibility of delivering a baby in the breech position.

The husband was looking on anxiously. "Is something wrong?" he asked.

Abigail turned to her mother, "Tell Dad to call the EMTs from the house phone. And bring a cell phone out here."

Karin explained to the husband, "The baby's bottom is coming first instead of the head. Usually . . ." She started to say that in the hospital the doctor would do a cesarean section, but Abigail sent her a warning glance.

Abigail asked the young woman, "What's your name?"

The woman held up her hand, motioning that she had a contraction. She caught her breath and said, "Beth."

"Beth, we'll keep you warm and dry until the EMTs can get here."

Abigail turned to the husband, "And what is your name?"

"Bill," he said.

"My name is Abigail. I'm experienced in delivering babies, but I would like to get your wife to the hospital."

At that moment, Beth had another contraction and she began to push involuntarily. Rita came back into the sauna, her face reddened and showing concern. "Dad talked to the rescue squad and it is impossible for them to get here in the next hour. There are electric lines down across the road. We wouldn't make it to the hospital either if we tried to drive."

"Then we'll help Beth give birth here," Abigail said. Mary had followed Rita to the sauna. When Abigail saw her, she beckoned to her. "I am going to need a couple things from my bedroom. I think I have a couple of hemostats and bandage scissors in the leather bag in my room. Could you find them and boil them for twenty minutes? If you could bring those, that would be great. Oh, and bring some orange juice for Beth."

"Mom, please get Dr. Larson on the cell phone. Tell him what is happening so he can advise."

Karin's stomach was in knots. How would they manage without the equipment available in the hospital? Beth moaned and grunted. Abigail returned to her side. She asked Bill to sit behind Beth and support her. Beth rested her back against Bill and bent her legs. Her heels were resting on the floor.

Abigail encouraged her to push with the contraction. "That's it. You are doing great. The baby will be here soon." Abigail looked at Karin with an expression of confidence. "I will need you to assist me. Get the dry towels from the sauna bench. They should be warm."

While the women were busy with the birth, the men had hunkered down in the living room. Paul had built a fire in the fireplace that was giving off a little heat. Soft light from the fireplace and candles danced and flickered in the room.

Peter asked, "How are things going in the sauna?"

"Abigail has taken charge, and she has Karin to help her. Let's pray for them," John said. He led in prayer, "Heavenly Father, we ask that you will watch over the birth of this baby. Give Abigail the skill that she needs. Protect the health of this young mother. We give you thanks and praise."

Jim prayed also. Peter listened to his friend ask for God's help. Peter admired Jim's faith and counted him a true friend. Jim was the first person who had reached out to him when he transferred to Michigan Tech. They had a class together, and Jim invited him to join a group of guys for outdoor sports. They hiked with snowshoes in the winter and camped in the summer.

Jim enjoyed fishing and had some favorite streams. On one of their fishing trips, Jim explained what the Bible taught about Jesus. Because of Jim, Peter had come back to church and was learning what it meant to pursue faith in God.

While prayer was taking place in the house, Rita reached Dr. Larson on the cell phone and tried to explain the situation to him. "Ben, I don't have time to tell you why she is in labor at our house. The baby is breech, and Abigail says that she is close to delivering."

"She can't deliver a breech out there. Get her to the hospital!" Ben roared in the phone.

"Electrical wires are down. Emergency vehicles can't get here. You've got to help us. Please, Ben."

Rita said to Abigail, "Ben's asking if it is a frank breech."

"Tell him yes."

"Ben says that when the body delivers, make sure that you pull a loop of umbilical cord forward."

Beth was pushing with each contraction. Abigail encouraged her to rest between them. The minutes passed and everyone focused on each push that Beth gave, cheering her on. Then Beth gave a strong push, delivering the buttocks, and the legs followed. Abigail pulled a loop of umbilical cord forward.

Rita relayed the progress, and then said, "Ben wants me to hold the telephone up to you." Rita crouched down and held the telephone up to Abigail's ear.

Abigail listened and instructed Karin. "Hand me a towel." Abigail wrapped the towel around the baby's legs. She looked to Karin and said, "You need to give suprapubic pressure now." Karin placed the heel of her hand just above the midline of the pelvic brim, Beth's lower abdomen.

Abigail said to Beth, "When you get a contraction, I want you to push hard all the way through the contraction. We'll work with the contractions."

It was silent in the room while they waited for Beth's contraction. Beth said, "It's coming now."

"Push hard," Karin said, as she put pressure with the heel of her hand. Everyone watched as Abigail gently pulled down on the baby's body and then moved her fingers up the baby's back to reach the upper arm and pull it down. Then she lifted the baby's body upward and released the lower arm.

"Maintain the suprapubic pressure," Abigail said to Karin.

Abigail lowered the baby's body, and it made a slight rotation. When Beth began to push with the next contraction, Abigail lifted the baby's body up. Beth pushed. The baby was facedown, and Abigail said, "Here's the chin."

The baby's nose and forehead emerged. Everyone cheered when Abigail held the baby up. The baby cried, and Dr. Larson yelled, "Bravo!" loud enough for Abigail, Karin, and Rita to hear.

Rita was relieved to stand up and flex her arm, numb from her frozen position. Mary returned to the sauna with supplies. She stood in the doorway, taking in the scene, and a couple of tears slipped down her cheeks.

Abigail felt the umbilical cord. "It's still pulsating. His heart rate is good." The umbilical cord was still delivering oxygenated blood to the baby, assisting his transition to breathing on his own. Bill had tears of joy on his face. Beth was smiling and reached for her son. Abigail placed the baby in her arms.

Karin felt like she was participating in a movie. She never imagined that birth could take place like this. She had never seen a breech birth. And it took place without intravenous fluid, without medications. She had watched Abigail work calmly and was amazed by her steady hands.

"Skin to skin," Abigail said, and she helped Beth lift her shirt and remove her bra. Beth brought the baby close against her breast. The baby boy was becoming a rosy pink as he nestled against his mother.

Mary set down the scissors and hemostats that she had wrapped in a clean cloth. She had asked her dad to bring the orange juice. He was waiting outside the door of the sauna, and Mary took the pitcher of orange juice and a large glass from him. "Everything's okay. The baby is here," she said.

John grinned. "Praise God! I'll call the rescue squad and let them know."

Mary filled the glass with orange juice and gave it to Bill. "Help Beth drink this."

Rita took in the scene. Beth was smiling, glowing as she held her baby. The infant was cuddled up against Beth's breast. Bill stood to one side with his eyes fastened on the healthy baby.

"Did you find my hemostats and scissors?" asked Abigail.

Mary nodded and handed the packet to Abigail. As Abigail unwrapped the instruments she looked to her mother. "Could you find some sanitary pads, clean underwear, and a robe for Beth? And could you have Dad bring a chair and a footstool here?"

"I'm feeling some cramping now," Beth said. Karin checked her bleeding and said, "I think the placenta is ready now."

Abigail asked for one of the plastic trash bags and laid it between Beth's legs. She clamped the umbilical cord about an inch from the baby's navel and placed the second hemostat a couple of inches away. She handed the scissors to Bill and showed him where to cut the cord between the hemostats.

"Okay Bill, can you hold your son? Take your shirt off and hold him against your chest. Skin to skin contact is good for him." Bill put down the half full glass of orange juice and removed his shirt. Abigail handed the baby to him and he held the baby cautiously at first and then cuddled him against his chest.

The baby fastened his eyes on Bill's face, and Bill touched the baby's hand, taking in the wonder of his baby boy. "Hello baby, I'm your dad."

Abigail focused her attention on Beth. She held the loose umbilical cord and applied gentle tension. "You can bear down now," she said to Beth. Beth pushed and the placenta slid out. Karin watched Abigail's actions intently.

"Karin, massage the uterus," Abigail said. Karin placed her hand on Beth's abdomen and felt for the uterine muscle. She massaged and felt it harden into a tight ball.

"It's firm," Karin said. Then she took Beth's pulse. "Her pulse is eighty-eight and strong."

"Make sure Beth finishes the glass of orange juice, and then pour her a second glass. It will help her uterus contract and prevent bleeding," Abigail said.

Karin looked dubious but followed Abigail's directions. She had depended on medications for uterine contraction in the hospital. Abigail wrapped the placenta in the plastic bag and slipped it into another bag. The shower room had everything they needed to clean up.

Rita returned with the requested sanitary pads, underwear, and robe. John and Paul brought a rocking chair and an empty plastic crate. "We didn't have a footstool but thought this crate might serve your purpose." They glanced briefly at the birth scene and then made a quick exit.

Karin and Abigail helped Beth wash up and put on the pads and clean underwear. Then they assisted Beth in getting upright, slipped the robe on her, and had her walk across the room. They seated her in the rocking chair and helped her put her feet up on the crate. Rita had brought a clean beach towel, and they laid this on her lap. Bill handed her the baby. Beth was radiant as she looked down on her newborn son. He was nuzzling her and opening his mouth.

"I think he's ready to breastfeed," Karin said. Karin took in the scene with pride and joy. She had participated in something wonderful. Beth looked strong. It was hard to believe that she had just given birth.

"Support your breast and touch your nipple to his mouth," Abigail instructed. The baby mouthed the breast and then sucked vigorously. Beth had a startled expression on her face. "Wow, he has a strong suck!"

"I'll stay here," Abigail said to the other women. "If there is any of that chili left, maybe you could bring a bowl for Beth and Bill."

With the news of the baby's healthy birth, the mood at the house became light. The men sat by the fire, talking football. The Detroit Lions had given them little to cheer about, but they were looking forward to the Rose Bowl. The University of Michigan would face the University of Southern California.

"Of course, it's a little hard for me to cheer for U of M, since I went to Michigan State for a couple of years," Peter said.

"But you would prefer Michigan to California, wouldn't you?" Paul said.

"When you put it that way, I have to go along with you. I love Michigan, especially the UP."

"Yeah, you have made a nice transition to our country life," Jim said.

"Lake Superior and the forests have grown on me," Peter said.

"Abigail is drawn to the copper country too; well, she has roots here. For a while we thought she might stay in Africa," Jim said.

"She has a nice opportunity to practice with Dr. Larson," Peter said.

"I was surprised when Dr. Larson relocated here. He left a partnership in Chicago to practice at Harbor Hospital and the regional medical center," Jim said.

"I wonder what the city girl thinks about our country life," Peter said.

"You mean Karin?" Paul said. "She looks like she's having a good time with Mary and Abigail."

Jim glanced at Peter. "Do I detect an interest in the fair maiden?"

The men heard the back door open. When Rita paused at the family room doorway, they all looked up attentively. Peter asked, "How are mother and baby?"

Rita said, "They are doing great."

"Do you think I could take a couple of pictures?"

"If they give you permission, it's okay. And if you are going to submit them to the newspaper, be sure to let them know."

Peter grabbed his camera and headed out to the sauna.

It didn't take long to warm up the chili. Rita carried two bowls out to the sauna. When she got there, Peter was still taking pictures. Abigail said, "Okay, the photo shoot is over. Beth needs to eat."

When the rescue squad arrived, John brought them out to the sauna. Beth and Bill were finishing their chili while Abigail held the baby and crooned to him.

The firemen laughed. "Everything is in order here—you don't need much rescuing. When you're done eating, we'll get you bundled up and take you to the hospital."

John asked, "How extensive is the power outage?"

"Parts of Hancock are out. Some outlying areas—like yours—are out. Calumet and Mine Harbor are okay. It may take a day or two to make the necessary repairs."

Abigail looked to Mary. "Is it okay if I stay at your place?"

Mary nodded, "What about you, Aunt Rita, and Uncle John?"

Rita looked to her husband and John responded, "We'll be okay here. Some extra blankets on the bed—and we can still make cowboy coffee on the gas stove. We'll be fine."

Peter thanked the Aaltios for their hospitality and asked Karin how long she was going to be around. Karin explained that she needed to drive back the following day. Since she had come with Abigail, she was hoping that Mary would drive down with her and spend a few days.

"So, you need a ride. I wouldn't mind making a trip to Chicago, and I can get off work Monday and Tuesday," Peter offered. "I could drive you."

Mary overheard Peter. "Are you serious? That would be good. I was having some misgivings about traveling on the winter roads."

Karin made a face at Mary. "Do I have a say in this? I thought you wanted to spend a few days with me."

"I do, Karin, but it would work out better if I came at another time with Jason. He can't go with us now."

Peter bowed. "So, may I have the pleasure of getting you to Chicago?"

Chapter 15

A sauna was clean—exceptionally so—from the heat, steam, and soap and water. The warmth brought relaxation as well as cleanliness so that the sauna was actually an ideal place for giving birth.

—*Of Finnish Ways*

ALIISA'S LABOR STARTED on a day when a light snow was falling steadily. The snow came down in soft, swirling flakes, adding to the white cover over the earth. Aliisa noticed brief contractions coming several times in an hour. Jan was away at the lumber camp. It was two weeks before her due date; the midwife was planning to come and stay next week. Pushing aside panicky thoughts, Aliisa began making preparations. She needed to send a signal to Hanna.

She set about building a fire in the old smoke sauna with the help of her oldest son. She stood by as Jeremy built the fire; she could not bend low enough to access the fire pit. They filled the large metal tub, which rested on the stones, with water. Throughout the day Jeremy visited the sauna and maintained the flames. The gray plumes of smoke made him cough as he stoked the fire. The sauna stones became hot and heated the water in the tub. Smoke billowed out of the vents along the roof of the sauna. It looked like the building was on fire. Hanna knew sauna smoke on a weekday was a sign that Aliisa was in labor. Hanna would send for the midwife.

Aliisa prepared food for the children and gave instructions to Jeremy for supervising the little ones. As the day progressed Aliisa paced and then rested in the rocking chair. The contractions were becoming stronger, and she wondered if Hanna had noticed her signal. With one strong contraction she bent forward, grabbing the back of a chair for support. She was about to send Jeremy out to get help when Hanna arrived on skis.

Hanna was surprised that the midwife hadn't come yet; she assured Aliisa that a message had been sent. Hanna would have come sooner, but one of her children was sick. When she observed the intensity of Aliisa's contractions, she set about organizing supplies for the birth.

Late in the afternoon, the fire in the sauna died out, and the walls and mound of stones resonated with heat. The smoke dissipated. As daylight faded, Aliisa and Hanna carried towels and blankets out to the sauna. The smoke was gone, and the benches were clean. Aliisa paused for a contraction, bending forward and resting her hands on the upper bench. She was grateful for her friend's presence.

The quiet peace in the sauna allowed Aliisa to release her body to the current of contractions. Gradually Aliisa stripped off her clothes. In the quiet darkness of the sauna she groaned and prayed for strength. She gave herself to this work of bringing a new life into the world. The contractions increased in intensity, and she cried out. Her body began to push with the contractions, and Aliisa relinquished control.

She gave a great push as she squatted, one arm braced on the sauna bench. Hanna caught the baby girl and placed her in Aliisa's arms. Aliisa's hair was damp with sweat and clung to her forehead and cheek. Her legs were streaked with blood. She held the baby close and wept with relief. Hanna was helping to dry the infant with a towel when the midwife pushed open the sauna door, calling out, "I'm here, Aliisa. Are you okay?"

The cry of an infant greeted her ears, and the midwife set about helping Aliisa with the afterbirth and recovery. Hanna went back to the house to prepare a meal for Aliisa and to check on the children.

Once Aliisa was cleaned up, the midwife assisted her in walking back to the house. She tucked Aliisa and the baby, Marja, into a clean bed and served the meal Hanna had fixed. She stayed with Aliisa for the next four days, managing the household and monitoring Aliisa's recovery. On the weekend, Jan would meet his new daughter.

Chapter 16

ABIGAIL, MARY, AND Karin were having a late-night cup of tea at the duplex. Karin asked questions about the birth they had just witnessed and expressed her admiration of Abigail's skill. "Was this your first breech delivery?" Karin asked.

"I witnessed one in Kenya," Abigail said.

"You were so calm," Karin said.

"It really helped to have Dr. Larson on the phone," Abigail said. "The baby needed to make rotations as it moved down the birth canal. He was telling me how to assist the baby's movement."

"It was amazing to watch the baby's arms and then face emerge." Karin was mentally reviewing the whole event. "Why did you insist that Beth drink orange juice?"

"It helps replace fluid and electrolytes, and that assists the uterine muscle to contract. Having a woman stand, take a few steps, and sit up also helps the body recover," Abigail said. She was touching on wisdom that midwives had learned over the years.

"It surprised me—this is so different from my experience."

"A woman's body is designed to give birth. Most of the time she just needs supportive care."

Beth's labor and birth was a vivid picture of the miracle of birth. The experience would stay with Karin. She felt a new energy and interest in her job as a labor and delivery nurse.

Karin toyed with her teacup and brought up the subject that was on her mind. "Peter is an interesting person, but I'm nervous about a long drive with him. I'm surprised that he offered to do this."

"Peter is a little eccentric, but he is easy to be with. You just have to get used to his camera—I don't think I have ever seen him without it," Mary said.

"Does he have a girlfriend?"

"No, not to my knowledge. Once Jim tried to set up a double date, including Peter, but it didn't happen."

Karin sipped her tea and wondered about the trip home. One more new experience was before her. Tomorrow was going to be an adventure.

The next morning Peter drove up in his old blue Mercury. Karin had forgotten about his car. Now she eyed the car suspiciously. "This is going to get us safely to Chicago?"

"Sure. If we have any problems I have a trunk full of tools," Peter said.

They talked about the wolf and the sauna birth during the first part of the trip.

Karin's ankle was steadily improving, and she was willing to reflect on the outing to the Hanka homestead. She acknowledged that it had been fascinating to see the wildlife. Peter said he had gotten some great photos.

"You seem pretty handy with the camera," Karin said.

"I got some neat pictures of that couple who gave birth in the sauna."

"That was an amazing experience," Karin said. "I admire Abigail, but I'm not sure what I think about her."

"What do you mean?"

"She is so sure of herself."

"She handled that birth with skill, but she had great support. It's a good thing you were there too. And the guys were praying for you," Peter said.

"Really?"

"Yep. While you were out in the sauna, John led us in prayer."

There was a period of quiet as Karin thought about Peter's comments. The men were praying for the women; that was a new concept. Her thoughts were interrupted when Peter turned on the radio. He channel surfed and picked up a local station. Reception lasted for about half an hour and then dissolved into static. He turned the radio off.

"Will your roommate be at home when we get to Chicago?"

Karin stared at Peter. "My roommate died a couple of months ago."

Peter glanced at Karin, not sure what to say. "I'm sorry. I guess I missed that piece of information."

Karin drew a deep breath. How could Peter know? She had talked about it, but had she ever said anything in Peter's presence? Karin wished the subject hadn't come up. She really didn't want to talk about it anymore.

Finally Peter asked, "What happened?"

Karin told her story briefly. And then she added, "Everybody thinks Lori was a fool to take pills to abort a pregnancy. But you know what, her boyfriend walked away when she became pregnant. The jerk walked away and didn't have the guts to come to her funeral," Karin said.

"How do you know that Lori's boyfriend knew she was pregnant?"

Karin was taken by surprise, and for a minute she didn't respond. "But he broke up with her. That was the reason they broke up."

"Are you sure?"

The next hour was awkward. Peter didn't know how to pick up the conversation. Finally, Karin fell asleep. She awoke when Peter pulled up to a Subway shop just past Green Bay.

"I thought we could stop for a sandwich. I need to stretch," Peter said.

Karin nodded. They were at a little strip mall with wide-open fields around them. The sound of cars and trucks on the freeway provided the background. Karin was glad to get out of the car.

When they sat down in one of the booths with sandwiches and soft drinks, Peter said, "I'm really sorry about your roommate."

"It's okay, I'm just a little touchy," Karin said. She was anxious to change the subject. "So how long have you known Mary's brother?"

"We had a couple classes together at Tech. That was three or four years ago. Jim's a really good guy."

"I like Mary's family and the Aaltios," Karin said.

"They are good, solid people. One more reason that I like the UP," Peter replied.

"My grandmother grew up near Mine Harbor. I like to think that her family was like Mary's."

"So you have roots there?"

"Recently discovered roots. When my grandmother died I got a case that contained family history stuff. You know, letters and pictures. And a receipt from the Finnish Steamship Company."

"Who came over from Finland?"

"My great-grandmother, I think. It was dated 1902."

"If you want to do a little research, there are a couple of sites on the Internet where you can track her emigration from Finland." Peter had assisted people who were doing genealogy research at the Tech library.

"So do you have a Finnish connection also?" Karin said.

"Nope. My dad's family was Swedish." Peter looked at his watch. "Well, time to get going. We should make it to Chicago while there is still some daylight."

When they arrived at Karin's apartment, Peter tried calling a friend. The friend wasn't in, and Peter turned to Karin. "Are you hungry? We could get some dinner, and I'll try Bob again in a couple of hours."

"There's a Thai restaurant a couple of blocks from here. We could get some take-out," Karin suggested.

"Sounds great."

They walked to Thai House and got a double order of chicken pad thai. When they returned to Karin's apartment, she adjusted the thermostat and cleared off the little table in the kitchen. She set the table and put a kettle on for hot water while Peter unpacked the white take-out containers. "It smells good," Peter said.

"My favorite comfort food," Karin replied.

They sat at the little table with their coats still on.

"This is something I can't get in upper Michigan. No Thai restaurants in Houghton or Hancock."

They savored the meal. As they finished eating, Karin offered Peter tea. Peter sipped his tea and then excused himself. He put another call through to Bob, and this time Bob was in. His conversation was short.

"Well, Karin, I'm going to head out. I have some photos to show Bob, and he has offered me his couch for the night."

It had been a long day. Peter thought about Karin as he drove to Bob's apartment. He wanted to get to know this woman with the deep brown eyes. He felt drawn to protect her, but the chaff of a previous relationship swirled around him.

During college his girlfriend had become pregnant. But she didn't tell him until after she had an abortion. Peter had been hurt and confused. He didn't understand why Brenda hadn't told him about the pregnancy. It was something that they should have talked about. They should have made a decision together.

The abortion had been more difficult than his girlfriend imagined; she was depressed and Peter didn't know how to relate to her. Eventually, they broke up. Peter transferred from Michigan State to Michigan Tech. He hadn't dated anyone since.

Lori's story had brought back buried memories. The scene played out in his mind. It was his sophomore year of college. Brenda was out of contact for a couple of weeks, not answering the phone, not responding to e-mail. She said she had been sick when he finally caught up with her.

"So sick that you can't answer the phone?" he asked.

Her lip quivered. "I had an abortion."

The statement rocked him back on his heels. Wasn't she using the birth control pill? He was stunned.

"Why didn't you tell me you were pregnant, Brenda?"

"I went to a clinic. It was supposed to be safe and easy."

"I thought you were taking the pill."

"I missed a day. I never thought this could happen," Brenda said. Her eyes were sad, her face lined with misery.

Peter was distressed by the situation but did not recognize his responsibility. Brenda messed up her birth control. And she didn't tell him that she was pregnant. Her depression was her own problem.

Brenda withdrew and built a defensive wall around her emotions. She had sacrificed so much for Peter. She had the abortion because they weren't ready to have a baby. Peter didn't comprehend that she was trying to keep their relationship the same. From Peter's perspective, she had changed. Peter and Brenda drifted apart.

Chapter 17

KARIN AWOKE TO the phone ringing. She sat up, cleared her throat, and picked up the phone. "Hello."

"Hello, Karin. It's Evelyn Larson. I hope I'm not waking you up."

Karin glanced at the clock. It was 9:30 a.m. "No, not at all," she lied.

"Ben dug up some information for you. Dr. Smith worked out of an abortion clinic in Chicago. I can give you the address if you have pen and paper."

"Just a moment!" Karin said as she scrambled out of bed and darted into the kitchen to grab a pen and notepaper. She went back to the phone and wrote down the information.

"Thanks so much. How did Dr. Larson find this out?"

"He still has quite a few connections in Chicago—he made some phone calls," Evelyn said. "He also suggested that you e-mail the FDA with information about Lori's illness and death after taking misoprostol. They have a program called MedWatch. Doctors, pharmacists, and concerned individuals can report a drug reaction." Evelyn gave her the web site.

"Okay, thanks," Karin said.

"How was your trip home?"

"Fine."

"I know you have a good job in Chicago but we'd love to have you consider Mine Harbor. Our little hospital needs good nurses."

"Thank-you," Karin said with feeling. Evelyn's warmth came through over the phone. Karin wondered if relocating to Mine Harbor was worth considering.

"Karin, we're praying for you. You've been through a tough time."

"Thank-you for everything," Karin said as she hung up. There was that word, prayer, again. Encounters with prayer were increasing.

Evelyn's words seemed genuine. It's like I really matter to her, Karin thought as she walked back out to the kitchen. She studied the address Evelyn had given her. It seemed familiar. Wasn't it one of the addresses that she had visited with Jenny? She put the slip of paper down.

As she made a pot of coffee, she thought about Peter. She liked him and he was unattached. That added some points to the idea of relocating. What would it be like to live in Mine Harbor? She turned her thoughts to getting organized for the day.

She added the information from Evelyn to the notes she had previously made and saved the empty pill containers. She would plan a trip to Detroit.

As Karin was getting ready for work, Peter was showing Bob some of his pictures.

"If you put together a group of lighthouse pictures, they could be used for a calendar or a travel magazine. There is a lot of interest in lighthouses and their history."

As they talked, Peter jotted down ideas. He was hoping to increase his income with photography sales.

It was noon when he left Chicago. A part of him wished that he had more time with Karin, but the old relationship still weighed on him and made him fearful of getting close to anyone.

He drove northward, stopping only for gas and a drive-through at a fast-food restaurant. A light snow was falling, and the roads were slippery in places. Peter was glad to be engrossed in his driving. It pushed all other thoughts from his mind.

He arrived late at night, went to bed, and slept. He was up early Tuesday morning and opened the daily newspaper. A picture he had taken of Beth, Bill, and their newborn infant was on the front page. Underneath was the caption, "Birth in the Sauna." A brief story accompanied the photo.

Peter studied the picture. There was something sacred about the bond between Beth, Bill, and their infant. He had felt the glow of joy in the sauna when he snapped the pictures. He felt a pang of guilt. Would he have married Brenda if she had told him that she was pregnant? He didn't know. He wondered what had happened to Brenda.

He put the newspaper down and made a pot of coffee. His thoughts drifted to Karin. One of the pictures he snapped of Beth included a lovely profile of Karin. She might enjoy seeing a copy of the newspaper. He could send her one. He felt safe keeping in touch with Karin from a distance. After a bowl of dry cereal and a cup of coffee, he went to his office at Michigan Tech.

A week later, Mary's brother Jim stopped by his apartment. "I'm glad you're alive. I've been trying to call you."

"Come in. Want something to drink?" Peter ushered Jim into his tiny kitchen and opened his refrigerator. "Take your pick."

Jim took a can of Coke, walked back to the living area, and sat down on the worn futon. The apartment held the essentials for living: a computer, a stack of books, and Peter's photography equipment. A picture of Torch Lake, taken during peak fall colors, was hanging on the wall. The linden trees around the lake were ablaze in gold and orange hues.

"How was your trip?" Jim asked.

"Trip?" Peter looked blank.

"To Chicago," Jim prompted.

"Oh, fine."

"Karin's seems like a nice girl," Jim said.

"Yeah."

Jim studied Peter. "You seem distracted. Something on your mind?"

Peter pressed his lips together. "Yeah, it's crazy. I haven't thought about this in a long time, but now it's bugging me."

"Do you want to talk about it?" Jim asked.

Peter hesitated. Jim waited. There was a long period of silence. "I don't know," Peter said.

"I'm your friend," Jim said.

"No one knows about this," Peter said.

"I can listen," Jim said.

Peter hesitated and finally said, "I don't know why I'm talking about this." He paused and then continued. "When I was in school downstate, I had a girlfriend. We were intimate and she became pregnant. I thought she was on birth control pills."

Jim silently waited for Peter to go on.

"She didn't tell me about the pregnancy until after she had an abortion. Then we split up. I haven't thought about this in a couple of years. I don't know why I'm thinking about this now."

"It's a painful memory," Jim mused. "Maybe God wants you to clear it up."

"What do you mean?" Peter asked.

"Sometimes we need to get rid of the sludge from our past in order to grow. I think I can explain it better with a Bible. Do you have a Bible?" Jim said.

Peter rummaged through a couple stacks of books against the wall and came up with a worn paperback copy. He handed it to Jim.

Jim opened the book to 1 John 1. He handed the Bible back to Peter
and said, "Read verses eight and nine."

Peter took the Bible and scanned the text.

If we claim to be without sin, we deceive ourselves and the truth is
not in us. If we confess our sins, he is faithful and just and will forgive
our sins and purify us from all unrighteousness.

Peter looked up, "You think that I am dealing with sin?"

"God designed the relationship between a man and a woman to be
good. Sex unites a man and a woman as one flesh. It is designed for marriage. Both men and women need to know and follow God's guidelines.
As humans we mess up in lots of ways, and then we hurt ourselves or
other people. Peter, I mess up. I have to confess my sins to God."

Peter listened, struggling with the concept of sin and forgiveness.
He thought about Jim's words after Jim left. He thought about Brenda's
depression and the downward spiral of their relationship. He had let
her take the pill. He never dreamed that she would become pregnant.
He had had not been committed to her but instead engaged in a selfish
sexual intimacy. He had not protected Brenda or even tried to help her
with the aftermath of the abortion. For the first time, the enormity of
his selfishness hit him and he wept.

He wanted the pain of this burden lifted. He wanted to follow God's
ways. Could God really forgive him? On his knees he confessed his sin
to God and asked for forgiveness.

A sense of peace followed, along with a desire to contact Brenda.
What would he say? I'm sorry? He hoped that Brenda had healed.

He sat with his laptop open. He struggled for words but finally sent
an e-mail to Brenda, expressing his sorrow for her pain. He *was* sorry.
The e-mail came back to him. The address was no longer valid.

Chapter 18

KARIN WENT IN to the hospital for a staff meeting, followed by an in-service. As she left, it so happened that Dr. Cutter was leaving the hospital at the same time. "Hey, I'm free for the evening. How about you? Want to do dinner together?" he said.

Karin hesitated.

Dylan said, "There's a nice Mexican restaurant just a couple of miles from here. Come on. I'll bring you back to your car later."

Karin gave in and followed him to his car. Dr. Cutter drove a silver Porsche with black leather seats. "This is quite a car," Karin said as the mental picture of Peter's old Mercury came to mind.

"This is my baby," Dylan said. " If we were going on the expressway, I might be able to show you what this car can do."

"That's okay," Karin demurred. "I can enjoy a short ride."

The restaurant was decorated with brightly colored paintings. A hostess greeted them cheerfully and led them to a table. The white tablecloths and fresh flowers sparkled in the colorful atmosphere. A waitress brought menus and asked if they would like anything to drink.

Dylan ordered a beer and suggested Karin get the same.

Karin smiled and replied, "Just water."

They both ordered the house specialty, enchiladas. It was still early for dinner and service was quick. The waitress brought their drinks, and as Dylan sipped his beer, their conversation turned more personal.

"I didn't see you around over Thanksgiving," Dylan said.

"No, I was in Michigan," Karin said. She decided to tell Dylan about the birth in the sauna. The glow of the experience lingered. There was something beautiful about the birth that Karin had witnessed.

"You mean that this woman gave birth in a bath house? That must have been a mess!" Dylan guffawed and nearly choked on his food.

"Actually not. The midwife handled the situation very well. A doctor instructed her over the phone, and she delivered a breech presentation," Karin said.

"You're joking. She didn't deliver a breech," Dylan said as he pushed his glasses up on his nose.

"She did," Karin said and decided to leave it at that. She was annoyed and frustrated by Dylan's attitude.

Their meals came, and Karin focused on eating. Dylan asked if she had found a roommate. Karin explained that she had someone in mind. It reminded her that she needed to call Jenny about making a trip to Detroit. And that reminded her about the pills, the misoprostol.

"Did you know that misoprostol is the second part of the treatment called RU-486?" Karin asked.

Dylan's eyebrows went up. "I guess I've heard that."

"I think it contributed to my roommate's death," Karin said.

"Didn't you say the cause of death was septicemia." Dylan said.

"But the infection might have started with an abortion."

"What's the point in pursuing this?"

"To find out the truth. I don't want this to happen to another woman."

"Listen, women want doctors to deliver perfect outcomes whether they take care of themselves or not. When they don't want a baby, they want us to provide an abortion. When things don't go perfectly, they sue the doctor. Doctors are trying to give women what they want. Do we get any appreciation?"

Karin sat back, shocked by his outburst. He was a doctor, and he was supposed to defend women's health. What was this about appreciation?

Dylan continued, "Do you know what the cost of malpractice insurance is? The world isn't perfect, but women demand perfect outcomes." Dylan had started out with ideals. He was going to be an outstanding doctor. He wanted to be respected and beloved by women. He was looking for the attention and adulation that he had missed as a child.

When his debt escalated—medical school loans, car payments, and malpractice insurance—he needed to find ways to earn more money. Money flowed through his fingers like water.

Karin figured that he needed to understand women better. She was about to reply when the waitress approached the table.

"Any dessert for you tonight?" she asked.

"Not for me," Karin said.

"I hope you won't mind if I have some. Have a cup of coffee with me," Dylan said. He turned to the waitress, "We'll have one coconut flan and two cups of coffee."

Karin flushed as she gathered her thoughts to speak her mind. As the waitress went to place their order, she said, "If women were given more information—all the facts including potential side effects—maybe their expectations would be more realistic. Maybe they could make better choices."

Dylan just shook his head. He knew what women wanted. It was his job to provide what they wanted. Mistakes happened and malpractice lawsuits just complicated his job.

He was moonlighting at a clinic, earning extra money to pay his bills. A friend from his days as a resident doctor was the director of an abortion clinic. Dylan worked one day a week at the clinic for lucrative pay. He kept it quiet.

Dylan changed the topic of conversation. "Have you ever been to Miami?"

"No. I went to Florida a few months ago, but it was the gulf side." Karin said.

"I'm going to a conference, and I happen to have an extra plane ticket. Would you like to go?"

"Why take me?'

"I could show you a good time."

"What would I do?"

"You could spend time at the beach or at the hotel pool. In the evenings we could go out."

"When are you going?"

"First week of February."

It sounded good to Karin. To escape the snow, ice, and bitter wind and spend time on the beach. And maybe she could change his ideas about women. "I'll think about it," Karin said.

"Of course I will be taking care of most of the cost, but maybe you could pay part of the hotel," Dylan said. He gave her an intent look. "It's a great opportunity."

Karin swallowed hard. The money might be a problem. She was still adjusting to her rent without someone to split the cost. And she would need to buy some new clothes.

"Sunshine, sandy beach, seafood restaurants, five-star hotel. You don't want to miss it," Dylan said. He was hoping to get a quick response.

"Sounds wonderful, but I have to think about it.

They finished their coffee, and Dylan drove her to her car. He put his car in park, moved towards her, and cupped her chin in his hand. Although she felt butterflies in her stomach, an inexplicable warning flashed through her mind. She moved away from his touch.

She playfully blew him a kiss. "Thanks for dinner," she said. She slipped out of his car and headed for her own.

At home she picked up the phone and called Jenny. "You will never believe what just happened. A doctor I work with just invited me to go to Miami with him."

"Wow, are you going to go?"

"Well, I'm not sure."

"Free trip to Miami—I'd take it."

"Well, not exactly free. He wants me to pay part of the expenses."

"Really, that's kind of cheesy. What's he like?"

"Intelligent, really smart. Recently divorced. He drives a gorgeous Porsche," Karin said.

"Ah, maybe he has a load of debt. Think twice about this," Jenny replied.

"The other reason I called—I'm thinking about coming to Detroit. Could I stay with you?"

"Sure. Anytime."

Next Karin called Lori's mother. She explained that she wanted to come out to visit. Karin mentioned that she had more information about Lori's death. Mrs. Sander said Karin could come any weekend, as long as she called ahead.

Karin called Jenny back, and they made plans. They decided on the second weekend in December. Karin would stay with Jenny, and they would visit Lori's mother together. The train connection between Chicago and Detroit would make the trip easy.

As the train clattered along the rails in Indiana and Michigan, Karin paged through *O, the Oprah Magazine*. She thought about Dylan Cutter; her encounters with him were disconcerting. She enjoyed his attention and was impressed by his apparent wealth. But he also made her feel uncomfortable.

The magazine was open in her lap. She gazed out of the window, watching the approach of a small town. The rhythm of the train and the hum of voices lulled Karin into a drowsy respite. She sank back in her seat and closed her eyes.

She was a little girl again, standing by her mother's bedside. The hospital room was foreign and intimidating. Her mother's forehead was bandaged, and she was very still.

Her mother's hand lay on the bed sheet and Karin grasped fingers with a chubby fist. Anne smiled faintly. "Mommy, I want you to come home," Karin said. Anne was too weak to reply and Karin began to cry.

A nurse in a white dress picked her up and handed her to someone. "I think you should take her home," she said. Karin woke up with a start, grief caught in her throat. She took a deep breath as the conductor announced that they were arriving in Detroit. Karin gathered her bags and prepared to disembark, trying to shake the dream out of her thoughts.

Karin and Jenny visited Mrs. Sander on Sunday afternoon. They had called ahead, but when Mrs. Sander opened the door she was wearing a stained robe. The smell of alcohol was on her breath. "Hello, Karin," she said. She looked hard at Jenny. "Who's that?"

Karin was startled. It was afternoon, and it was obvious that Mrs. Sander had been drinking. "This is Jenny. She was one of Lori's friends."

"Come in," Mrs. Sander said, gesturing vigorously. The women entered the living room and were greeted by framed pictures of Lori. The coffee table was stacked with papers and some had slid onto the floor.

Mrs. Sander used to have a neat and well-ordered house. Cups and paper plates had been piled on an end table. Karin was shocked but said nothing. "Sit down, sit down," Mrs. Sander said.

Karin focused on one of the pictures of Lori. "That was our junior year."

"Homecoming—Lori loved that dress." Mrs. Sander said.

Karin exchanged a glance with Jenny, wondering whether to go ahead with sharing the information. She paused and Mrs. Sander asked, "So what do you know?"

Karin brought out the pill containers and explained how the medications were used. She explained the procedure for medical abortion and her theory.

Mrs. Sander looked down and then shook her head. "The doctor said she might have been pregnant. I didn't want that to come out. It's enough that I have lost Lori." She sobbed, her shoulders shaking. "Why are you bringing this up?"

"Lori may have had bad care from the clinic that prescribed these pills." Karin explained the chain of events and showed Mrs. Sander the pill containers and the dates on them. She explained the purpose of the medications and how they were linked to abortion.

"I think you should pursue this," Karin said. "Maybe your ex-husband could help you."

Mrs. Sander shook her head. "He don't care." Lori's mom was not herself.

"I'm sorry," Karin said. They sat in silence for a couple of minutes.

"Lori is all I had," Mrs. Sander began to sob and hiccough.

"I think you should pursue justice for Lori," Karin said. She gave Mrs. Sander the name and address of the clinic that had provided Lori's treatment. "Bring this information along with the death certificate to a lawyer. I think it's grounds for a lawsuit." Mrs. Sander gave Karin a blank look. Karin wasn't sure if she understood.

"At the least, the Food and Drug Administration should be notified. I could take care of that," Karin said.

"Okay, I guess."

"We would just need a copy of Lori's death certificate. Do you have more than one?"

Mrs. Sander nodded, "Yeah." She began sorting through the stack of papers. When she didn't find it, she looked at the papers on the floor.

"Do you mind if I help you look?" Karin asked.

"Okay," Mrs. Sander replied. "I know it's here somewhere."

Karin went through the papers slowly and eventually found several copies of the death certificate. "Do you mind if we take one?"

Mrs. Sander shrugged, "I guess that's okay."

The girls left, promising to return after stopping at an office supply store. They made copies of the information on the pill containers, the clinic address, and the death certificate. They bought two document envelopes and placed Mrs. Sander's copies in one, their own copies in another.

They brought the envelope to Mrs. Sander and encouraged her to contact a lawyer. She said, "Sure." Her eyes were a little bloodshot. She laid the envelope on top of the stack of papers. Then she sank down on a chair and picked up her drink.

Out in the car, Jenny asked Karin, "What do you think? Will she do anything with the information?"

"I don't know. But at least we have information to inform the FDA. Evelyn Larson gave me the web site."

When they reached Jenny's apartment, Jenny opened up her computer. After the women filed a report with the FDA, they talked about Mrs. Sander. Karin was concerned about the change she saw in her. She made a mental note to contact Mrs. Sander again.

Jenny began talking about springtime. She explained her plan to get a job in Chicago. "Would you like a new roommate?"

"My lease is up in April," Karin said.

"Perfect. We could apartment hunt together." Jenny was looking forward to a change, and Karin welcomed the idea of having a roommate.

When Karin returned to Chicago, she found a message in her mailbox. The post office was holding a package for her.

Chapter 19

THE PACKAGE TURNED out to be a manila envelope too large to fit in the mailbox. Karin looked at the return address and was surprised to see that it was from Peter.

She opened it and found a Christmas card and a copy of the *Harbor Herald*. She smiled with pleasure when she noticed a picture of the sauna birth. Peter had also included a carefully wrapped five-by-seven picture of herself with Beth and the baby. She shook her head in amused wonder. He had taken a lot of pictures. The camera was like an appendage on Peter.

She studied the images. Peter was a talented photographer. She read the newspaper article, which included a quote from John Aaltio: "I had read stories about Finnish women giving birth in the sauna. This past weekend a birth took place in ours. We were blessed to be a part of it."

Karin was not in the habit of sending Christmas cards, but she made a special effort to buy one for Peter. Something about Peter warmed her heart. She wrote a short letter and paused with pen in hand, trying to express her thanks. She crumpled up the first copy—tried again and tossed the paper in the garbage. She read over the third attempt, folded it, and slipped it in with the Christmas card.

The week before Christmas, she noticed a large stone church on her way to work. The sign in front displayed the notice of a ten o'clock service on Christmas morning. Perhaps going to church would make the day a little more special.

The day arrived, and Karin dressed up in a ruffled blouse and wool slacks. She put on her winter coat and slipped out the door. She was outside for two minutes when she came back to the apartment for a hat, a scarf, and gloves. The temperature hovered in the teens, and the wind packed a punch of freezing air.

When sufficiently bundled, she headed for her car and drove to the beautiful stone church with a bell tower. On entering the foyer, she noticed the Christmas tree with golden trimmings. A smiling usher offered her a bulletin. The sanctuary of the church was decorated with holly and huge poinsettias. She sat down taking in the richness of the holiday decorations.

The scripture readings and hymns were celebratory. Karin sensed the joy being expressed, but she also felt very alone. It was like she was viewing a window scene.

Couples and families were in attendance, but she didn't know one person. The families sat together in tight huddles. She slipped out of church as soon as the service was over.

As she walked to her car, Mrs. Sander came to mind. She wondered how she was doing this first Christmas without Lori. Like herself, Mrs. Sander was probably lonely. She decided to call her before going to work.

It sounded like she had awakened Mrs. Sander. Her voice was thick and slow.

"Who is this?" she asked.

Karin gave her name, and then said, "Remember? I'm Lori's friend."

"Okay, that's right."

"I'm calling to wish you a merry Christmas," Karin said.

"Thank-you."

"Do you have plans for the day?"

"Oh, I have my favorite TV dinner. It's just me here." She gave a forced laugh.

Karin told her about the church service she had attended. Mrs. Sander was silent, and Karin continued to make conversation, talking about her job. She explained that she was going to work the evening shift.

"It's nice you'll be with some people," Mrs. Sander finally said.

"Have you contacted a lawyer yet?" Karin asked. Karin had called her a week ago, and although Mrs. Sander expressed interest in legal help, she had not pursued it.

"I don't know who to talk to," Mrs. Sander said with a sigh.

Karin had barely put the phone down when it rang. It was her dad calling to give his greetings. "I wish you were home, sweetie. I miss you."

"Well, you know. It's the way it is. Nurses have to work the holidays," Karin said.

"Did you get my card with the check?" Mr. Lindale asked.

"Yes, thanks. I'm saving it for the after-Christmas sales. What are you doing today?"

"I'm going to enjoy a quiet day. I leave on a business trip tomorrow."

"Have a good day, Dad. I love you." Karin wanted to keep the call short. She didn't want her emotions to spill out. She turned her attention to getting ready for work.

The day after Christmas, Mary called. They chatted and exchanged news. Karin told Mary about her conversation with Mrs. Sander. "I don't know if she will find a lawyer."

"There should be information on the Internet," Mary suggested.

"I wish I had a computer. Maybe I can get to the library this week," Karin said.

Mary explained that she and Jason were planning to travel to Indiana the first week of January. "Is it okay if we come through Chicago and stay at your place for a night?"

Karin responded without hesitation. "Yes, of course. You can stay as long as you want!" The thought of friends at her apartment lifted her spirits.

Two days later Karin found time to get to the library. She did an Internet search for abortion malpractice. She found several websites and an 800 number for legal assistance. She wrote down the information and went home to call Mrs. Sander.

Mrs. Sander promised to call the legal assistance number. She sounded better on the phone and appreciated Karin's help.

A week later, just before Mary and Jason arrived, Mrs. Sander called. "The number you gave me was good. That office referred me to a lawyer in the Detroit area. Karin, you were right. The lawyer believes Lori received negligent care. He wants to meet with me and look over the information."

"I'm glad you're going ahead with this. Let me know if there is anything that I can do," Karin said. They talked for a while and Karin told Mrs. Sander about her friends, the newlyweds. She was looking forward to their visit.

Mary and Jason took Karin out to dinner. It was fun to catch up on news.

They told Karin that as they moved out of the duplex, Abigail moved in. She was happy to be closer to the hospital.

"By the way, how was your ride down from the UP with Peter?" Mary said.

"It was fine. I was wondering if he felt sorry for me—he seemed kind of distant. And then out of the blue, he sent me a Christmas card and a copy of the *Harbor Herald*," Karin said. "I can't quite figure him out."

Mary asked about Karin's job, and she mentioned Dylan Cutter. Mary was happy that Karin seemed to have a friend, but she had a pang of unease when Karin mentioned the invitation to Miami, Florida.

Chapter 4

"How much do you know about him?" Mary asked.

"He's a doctor, and he makes good money. Drives a silver Porsche," Karin said. She avoided telling Mary that he was divorced.

Mary listened to Karin thoughtfully. She knew Karin was hungry for friendship. She would pray for Karin and make efforts to stay in touch with her. It wouldn't hurt to encourage Abigail to make contact with Karin.

Back at the apartment, Mary sorted through her luggage and pulled out an envelope for Karin. "Aunt Rita sent this along with me. It's something that she translated for you."

"Oh, the letter. Gosh, I forgot about it." Karin put the envelope on the kitchen counter. "Thanks, I'll read it later."

The next morning Karin made a pot of coffee. She set out bagels and cream cheese. As she began pouring coffee, Mary said, "None for me."

"What, you've stopped drinking coffee? You started me on coffee," Karin said.

Mary had kept a pot of coffee going all the time when they were roommates.

"It's strange. Coffee doesn't appeal. Almost make me nauseous."

Karin studied Mary, "Are you pregnant?"

Mary looked startled and didn't speak for a minute. "My period *is* late . . . I guess it's a possibility."

When Jason entered the kitchen, he noticed the expression on his wife's face. "What's up?"

"Just girl talk."

When Mary and Jason prepared to leave after breakfast, Karin whispered to Mary, "Let me know," as she gave her a hug.

"I wish you had a computer. It would make it easier for us to keep in touch."

"It's on my list. I have to figure out my finances," Karin said.

After they left, Karin noticed the envelope on the counter and put it in her grandmother's Bible for safekeeping. She cleaned up the breakfast dishes and did a load of laundry.

As she got ready for work, she wondered if Dylan Cutter would be at the hospital. The unit was busy when she arrived, and she was immediately assigned to circulate for a repeat cesarean section. When the patient was moved into the recovery room, she continued to provide care and hooked up the monitors.

The patient had epidural anesthesia running, but it wasn't covering the pain. She moaned, and her face was taut and pale. Karin checked a reading of her vital signs and called the anesthesiologist.

He came to assess the patient and gave her a bolus of medication. "I have given the maximum amount." But after he left, the patient continued to complain of pain.

Her blood pressure was falling slightly. Karin checked the dressing on the incision and the pads under the woman. She didn't see any excessive bleeding. When she checked the uterus for firmness, it felt strange to her. It was firm but with a soft crinkly area in front of the uterus. She called the surgeon and explained her observations. He listened carefully to her description of the uterus and the patient's unrelenting pain.

"She may be bleeding internally," he said. He spoke with an urgent tone, telling her to order a stat CBC (complete blood count) and prepare to send the patient to surgery. Karin called the charge nurse and asked for help. The next ten minutes were a flurry of activity as they got the lab work, which showed a dropping blood count. Karin and the resident doctor rushed the patient to the main operating room. Karin had the extra energy of an adrenaline rush, and they moved through the halls at a fast pace. They pushed the stretcher onto an elevator, and Karin took a pulse. It was faint and fast. The patient said, "I feel a little dizzy."

Karin held her hand. "You're okay. Your doctor is going to take care of the problem. Rest back against the pillow."

The surgeon met them at the entrance to the operating room. Karin helped the OR nurse move the patient onto the operating table. Then she returned to her unit as the OR staff took over. Karin documented the whole event at the nurses' station. She was shaking as she wrote.

She was in the nurses' lounge drinking a cup of coffee with one of her coworkers when she was called to the nurses' desk. She walked out to find the patient's doctor waiting to thank her.

"Your observations helped me guess what was happening. The patient was bleeding out into her abdomen from a severed blood vessel. There were almost two liters of blood in the abdominal cavity. We're giving her blood. She'll go to ICU overnight for observation."

Dylan Cutter happened to enter the nurse's station at that moment and walked over to Karin. "Good job!" he said as he massaged her shoulders. The scent of Dylan's cologne was strong, and Karin wrinkled her nose.

She blushed and then asked, "How was your Christmas?"

"It was alright," he said with a flat expression that hinted it had not been all right.

The next day Dylan called her at home. "Karin, have you made up your mind about Miami?"

Karin sighed. "I don't think I can go. Money is tight for me."

"I'll take care of everything," Dylan promised.

Karin almost wavered but then held to her decision. She wasn't ready to spend days and nights with Dylan.

"Well, maybe we could go out for a drink after work one of these nights. Are you working on Friday?"

"Yeah, I'm scheduled for Friday."

"Okay, let's meet Friday night. Midnight okay?"

"That's fine."

Chapter 20

KARIN SAT AT Bailey's Bar and Grill. She had ordered hot cider and was waiting for Dylan to show up. She rested her chin on her raised arm and fist, elbows planted on the table, as she reviewed the events of a busy shift. Her dark, curly hair framed her face.

Dylan arrived and slid into a seat across from Karin. He ordered a drink and after eyeing her up and down, said. "You look great." It was hard for him to keep his eyes off the sweater that clung to her chest.

Karin blushed and crossed her arms. She felt uncomfortable.

"Aw, you're not embarrassed, are you? You have a lovely shape, sweetheart," he said. "How was work?"

"I was running between rooms. I had two deliveries, just an hour apart."

Dylan brought up the names of a couple of nurses on the maternity unit and critiqued their skills. He told a story about one nurse knocking over a tray of instruments. Karin swallowed her amusement and said sternly, "Don't make fun of my coworker."

Dylan changed the subject. He talked about an auto show and some of the snazzy vehicles he saw there. Karin nodded but found it hard to pay attention.

She struggled with her end of the conversation and suggested that it was time to head home. Dylan walked out to the car with her. He pulled her into a tight embrace and kissed her. Karin struggled to free herself.

"Please Dylan, let me go."

Dylan let go reluctantly. Karin breathed a sigh of relief and was thankful that she was not joining him for the trip to Miami. She drove off, anxious to get back to her apartment.

On the weekend Karin was sitting up, flipping channels on TV, when she received a call from the night charge nurse. Carla explained that they had five new admissions and the staff was overwhelmed. Could she come in and help out for a few hours?

Karin couldn't sleep. She might as well go in to work. She told Carla that she would be there in a half hour.

Carla greeted her with a smile and words of gratitude. She handed her a clipboard. "Jean just put a patient in labor room five. Get report from her and finish the admission."

Jean had been a labor and delivery nurse forever. Her white hair was thin and limp. She was built sturdily and had a few extra pounds. When Karin entered labor room five, Jean looked up. "Angela has a fever and is contracting. I'm putting her on the monitor. Go get IV fluids and start her IV."

When Karin first started at Northland Hospital, she had been afraid of Jean. Jean gave orders, she criticized, and she pushed the new nurses to grow. Whenever she oriented a nurse, she gave her a hard assignment, but she backed her up. Eventually Karin came to respect Jean and found she could learn a lot from her. She went to get supplies and admission forms.

It was several hours before there was a pause in the frantic activity of caring for the new admissions. When Karin finally sat down at the nurses' station, Carla commented, "I'm so glad that I caught you at home." Carla paused and hesitated before continuing. "You know, someone said they saw you the other day at Bailey's with Dr. Cutter."

"Oh, really." Gossip traveled quickly around the unit.

Jean's head turned, and she gave Karin advice. "Be careful, Karin. He just went through a nasty divorce. You don't want to get involved with him."

"His private life is kind of a mess," Carla agreed.

The warnings upset Karin. She did not want to be the topic of conversation.

Over the next week, Karin did not encounter Dr. Cutter. She decided to put him out of her mind. She went to the library and picked up some books and magazines. She was enjoying a lazy morning, sipping orange juice, and reading a magazine, when she received an unexpected phone call.

The man introduced himself as a lawyer investigating Lori Sander's death. "I understand you were with her the last two days of her life. I am coming out to Chicago to see records at the hospital. I would like to have a chance to talk with you as well."

Karin was willing, and they set a date to meet at a Caribou Coffee. She was pleased that this lawyer was moving forward. She hoped it would bring closure for her.

Karin arrived at the coffee house a few minutes late on the appointed day. A man in a gray business suit was standing at the counter. As she approached he turned and looked her way. He appraised her for a moment and then asked, "Are you Karin Lindale?"

"Yes, you must be Don Anderson," Karin said as she extended her hand.

"What can I order for you?" Don asked.

Karin glanced at the blackboard with the daily offerings. "A large Kenyan coffee with cream and sugar."

When their drinks were ready, Don guided Karin to a booth along the wall.

He began with, "I'm sorry that your friend died. Can you tell me what happened? If you don't mind, I'd like to tape record your account."

Karin nodded, "That's fine."

Karin told him the sequence of events. Finding Lori sick, taking her to the hospital, visiting her, the transfer to the ICU.

"What was the span of time between when you found her and when she died?"

"It was less than twenty-four hours," Karin said.

"When you found her, you said that she had taken some medication," Don prompted.

"Yes, she said she had taken Tylenol with codeine for pain. The pill container was on the table next to her."

"Did she say why she was taking this medication?"

"She said it was for stomach cramps. I thought it was strange that she was taking a strong pain medication, was so weak, but couldn't tell me what was wrong. That alarmed me so I took her to the emergency room."

"When did you realize she had taken another medication in the week before she died?"

"It wasn't until after the autopsy, after the funeral. I found the pill container under the bed. I suppose Mrs. Sander showed you the pill containers?"

"Yes, she did. She also gave the address of the clinic you researched."

Karin smiled, "Actually some friends helped me discover that."

"I've been to the clinic. There are a couple of doctors at that clinic. Dr. Ken Smith and Dr. Dylan Cutter."

Karin paled. "What did you say?"

"There are actually two doctors at that clinic, Dr. Smith and Dr. Cutter. The clinic sees patients on Mondays, Wednesdays, and Fridays.

Coverage on the other days is sketchy. There usually is a receptionist there."

"Are you okay? Is something wrong?" Don looked at Karin quizzically.

"I may know one of the doctors," Karin said vacantly. Dylan never worked at the hospital on Friday. He talked about the high price of malpractice insurance and yet he drove a Porsche. Her heart sank.

"You know one of these doctors?"

"In another setting. I had no idea he worked at this clinic." She swallowed hard and forced herself to concentrate. It made her nauseated to think that she had talked about Lori with him.

"What happens if a patient needs the doctor and he is not available?" Karin asked.

"The receptionist assured me that the doctor is paged. I can see you're alarmed. Do you think Lori had difficulty reaching a doctor?"

"I don't know. I think she should have been seen after her pain escalated, but she said she got the prescription over the phone."

"I am going to do a little more research on the clinic," Don said. "And I will go over the records at the hospital."

"I guess you should know that one of these clinic doctors also works at the hospital where Lori died," Karin said.

The lawyer's eyebrows went up. "Did he know Lori was at the hospital?"

"I don't know."

Chapter 21

T WORK ON Thursday, Karin entered the elevator and almost ducked out when she noticed Dr. Cutter. He gave her an amused look and reached out to pull her close. "I don't bite," he said.

Karin returned his gaze steadily. "I was surprised to find out about your second job. I didn't know you worked at the clinic on First Avenue."

Dylan pushed his glasses up on his nose and stared at Karin. His expression tightened. "I don't know what you're talking about."

"Why can't you level with me? What kind of care did my roommate get at your clinic?"

"It's not my clinic, and I didn't treat her."

The elevator door opened before Karin could respond, and Dr. Cutter stalked out. Karin took a deep breath and headed to the nurses' locker room to change into scrubs.

Karin was upset when she learned that she had been assigned to Dr. Cutter's patient. She requested a change, but the charge nurse responded, "I'm sorry Karin, you'll have get through this shift. I can't redo the assignments now."

Karin sighed. The evening was off to a bad start. She took report on her patient and went in to introduce herself. The patient's labor was being induced, and she was restless. After checking vital signs, Karin did an internal exam and determined that the cervix was halfway dilated. She asked the patient if she needed pain medication. The young woman nodded. Her husband said, "She wants an epidural."

Karin turned to the woman who said, "Yes, an epidural."

Karin set the preparations in motion. She called Dr. Cutter for the order and had the patient sign a consent form. She gave a bolus of intravenous fluid, gathered the equipment for placing an epidural catheter, and paged the anesthesiologist.

Placement of the epidural was difficult. Karin helped the patient to a sitting position, encouraged her to round her back, and asked her to stay still. Whenever she had a contraction, she moaned and grabbed Karin's arms. Karin was trying to support her in good position.

"Karin, you need to keep her still," the anesthesiologist said.

Karin sighed and encouraged her to take slow deep breaths. "Stay very still and this will be done soon."

The procedure seemed endless as Karin tried to maintain accurate monitoring. The digital screen in the room showed the patient's heart rate, but an alarm beeped because the fetal heart rate was not being recorded. The ultrasound transducer was not in an optimum position, and Karin kept shifting it to pick up the baby's heart rate. The patient's husband was looking over her shoulder.

On the third attempt, the anesthesiologist placed the epidural catheter.

He gave a test dose of medication, and Karin set the timing for automatic readings of the patient's blood pressure and pulse. The anesthesiologist then gave a bolus of medication, and promised the patient that she would have pain relief in minutes. Karin helped the patient lie down on her back.

The monitor alarmed and displayed a drop in blood pressure. Karin opened the flow of intravenous fluid. "Her blood pressure is 84/42," Karin said.

"Give her ten milligrams of ephedrine," the anesthesiologist said.

Karin drew up the medication and pushed it slowly into a port in the intravenous tubing. She continued to monitor vital signs and the baby's heart rate. The anesthesiologist stayed around for fifteen minutes to gauge the pain relief and to make sure the blood pressure was stable. Then it was up to Karin to manage the patient's care. Karin had been in the labor room for an hour and a half.

She inserted a Foley catheter to drain urine because the patient could no longer sense the need to urinate. Karin stayed in the room, keeping up documentation and making observations for another half hour. She glanced at the fetal monitor as she started to leave for a quick break. The baby's heart rate was slowing down; the digital readout flashed seventy beats per minute. The patient's blood pressure had dropped again and was reading 80/40.

She turned off the induction pump and increased the rate of intravenous fluid. She reached for the emergency call button and began assisting the patient to turn to her left side. The charge nurse and OB tech rushed into the room. Dr. Cutter was on their heels.

"Should I give another dose of ephedrine?" Karin asked.

Dr. Cutter looked at the monitor strip, examined the patient, and said, "Yes, let's get her pressure up. And then get her ready for a c-section. The baby is stressed, and we need to deliver her."

While the charge nurse called the anesthesiologist and a surgical assistant, the OB tech raced to the operating room and began opening the surgical packs. Karin and the charge nurse pushed the patient's bed to the operating room, and together they assisted the patient onto the operating table. Within fifteen minutes the surgery was started.

A nursery nurse came to assess and care for the baby. Karin was responsible for making sure that the surgical team had everything they needed. She also documented the surgery and kept up the sponge and needle count. She made sure the patient's husband came into the room at the right time.

The communication between Karin and Dr. Cutter was brisk and abrupt.

The baby cried as he was lifted from the uterus. The mother looked to Karin, and Karin smiled. "He is pinking up," she said as the baby bawled. "Cathy is our nursery nurse and she will bring him over to you after the neonatologist checks him out."

The surgical team focused on closing the layers of uterus, muscle, fascia, and skin tissue. Karin kept her head down and filled in the surgical record. She avoided looking toward Dr. Cutter. She was anxious for this case to be over.

Dr. Cutter worked quickly, and as soon as he was done stitching, he left the operating room. It was up to Karin, the anesthesiologist, and the OB tech to move the patient onto a clean bed and bring her to the recovery room. The drape that caught blood and fluid had not been secured well, causing leakage onto the floor. Karin tossed towels on the floor and stepped cautiously. She fumed over the mess Dr. Cutter left.

The unit was very busy at that moment because two deliveries were in progress, so Karin continued to care for her patient in the recovery room. While she watched vital signs, she tried to complete her documentation of the labor care.

Finally, one of her colleagues was free to relieve her. Karin glanced at the clock. It was seven o'clock, and she realized with disappointment that the cafeteria was closed. She had not eaten anything since noon. Sometimes she brought a pack lunch to work, but not today. She would have to get something from the vending machines on the basement level.

She put on a cover gown and walked to the elevator outside of the maternity unit. She pressed the elevator button several times and finally decided to take the stairs. She ran down the steps without noticing a little water spill. The ankle that she had turned a couple of months ago gave in again. She lost her balance and tried to catch herself. She reached for the wall, missed, and came down hard on her right arm.

Pain shot through her arm as she lay in a crumpled heap. As she attempted to get to her feet, a male nurse entered the stairwell. He assisted her. "Are you okay?" he asked.

"I slipped," Karin said. She stretched out her arm. "I'll probably get a big bruise." She tried to smile but instead grimaced.

He waited a minute for her to get her bearing and opened the door to the basement corridor. "Looks like you've got the weight of the world on your shoulders."

"It's been a rough day." Karin said. "I'll be okay if I get something to eat." She thanked him for his help and went on to the vending machines. The sandwiches weren't particularly appealing, but she picked ham on wheat and a bag of potato chips.

She returned to her unit, wincing from the sharp pain in her arm. She had Tylenol in her locker and took a dose before going to the nurses' lounge to eat. When she went back to the nurses' desk, she found it difficult to type on the computer. The charge nurse asked her what was wrong, and Karin told her about her fall. The charge nurse looked at Karin's arm and asked her to move her fingers. Then she asked her to turn her wrist. Karin winced and bit her lip. The charge nurse insisted that she go to the emergency room.

Karin sat in the emergency room and tried to block the memory of her last visit there with Lori. Finally she was sent for an X-ray, which showed a break in the small bone of her arm just above the wrist. While the doctor applied a temporary cast, she asked, "How long will I need this on?"

"You'll need to see an orthopedic doctor tomorrow. He'll let you know." He gave her a referral. The day had started out bad and had ended worse.

The next day Karin called in sick and made her way to the doctor's office. He checked the X-rays and applied a permanent cast to Karin's right arm. He told Karin that her arm would be in a cast for at least five weeks. Karin groaned. At least she would receive workman's compensation.

Karin was depressed. She was going to have a lot of time on her hands. At another point in her life she might have been happy with the free time. Now she didn't know what to do with herself. It was lonely in the apartment.

She was glad to hear a friend's voice when Mary called. Karin spilled out her story, stopping occasionally to control her emotions. She didn't want to cry.

"Have you thought about going home for a while?" Mary asked.

"No, my dad is out of town most of the time. It doesn't make sense for me to go home," Karin said.

Karin turned the conversation away from herself. "How are things in Indiana?"

"It's fun to be on a large campus again," Mary said. "I have exciting news. You were right, and I am impressed that you picked up on it. I'm pregnant."

"Gosh Mary, that's great! Congratulations! When are you due?"

"The beginning of September."

They chatted for a little longer. Then Mary called Abigail and shared her concern about Karin. Mary and Abigail talked about encouraging Karin to travel and stay with friends. Mary said she would suggest that Karin come to Indiana.

"And I'll invite her to stay with me. I'm settled in the duplex now and have the extra bedroom," Abigail said.

Mary and Abigail both called Karin and asked her to come for a visit. At first she refused. She was feeling sorry for herself and pushed her friends away. I don't need people to pity me, she thought.

She was up late one night and pulled out her grandmother's Bible. She thumbed through it hoping for direction, but she didn't know where to begin. She found the envelope with the letter that Rita had translated. She had forgotten about it. She pulled it out and unfolded the yellowed paper with flowing cursive writing. The second sheet of paper was a typewritten translation of the Finnish words.

Dear Marja,

It's quiet on the farm with just your father and brother Jack here. We sold the last cow. Fido is a little forlorn with no cows to chase. He follows me around and lies at my feet whenever I sit.

The women's society of our church met again to fill boxes to send to Finland. The news continues to be bad. Our brave men are trying to hold the border against Russia.

I miss you and the long walks we took together. I know that you must pursue your dreams. You worked hard in high school; I was so proud of you at your graduation. It was hard to let you go, but I understand your decision to pursue a job in Detroit. There isn't much opportunity here.

When I was your age, I left Finland for a job in Calumet. When I first came, it was a bustling town and I was so happy. Can you imagine carriages, trolley cars, hockey games, and concerts in the park? Famous people, like Sarah Bernhardt, came to the Calumet Theater. It was an exciting place.

I worked in a beautiful house, and I looked forward to having one of my own. In my mind I had already picked out the drapes and wallpaper. I planned to invite my friends over for coffee, make use of the town library, and learn English.

That was my intention when I married Jan. The mines were prosperous. Surely Jan would earn enough to have a nice house in town. I didn't know much about the dangers of mining.

The miners arranged a strike to press for better working conditions. The situation got worse before it improved. Your father saw an opportunity to buy land, so he left the mines.

The first Great War started in 1914 and the demand for copper increased. For a little while the miners earned good wages. At first I was bitter. If Jan had stuck with it, he would have received better pay, but only for a brief time. Some of the mines shut down after the war.

God used that painful time to get my attention. Other families had subsistence farms. We began to meet together to pray, sing, and learn from the Bible. I needed God and the companionship of faithful friends. I began to see how God was providing for our family.

The joy of life that I thought was dependent on my plans was fulfilled in my relationship with the Lord God. I found peace and strength in our little church.

I hope that you will find Christian friends and a church. When the unexpected happens, you will need guidance from the Lord God.

I am praying for you and sending you a Bible. Study God's word and rest in his promises.

Love always,
Mother

Karin reread the letter. "Dear Marja"—this was a letter sent to her grandmother from Aliisa, probably not long after her high school graduation. The words crossed years of time and impacted Karin. She thought, this letter could apply to me.

Karin thumbed though the Bible. She noticed paragraphs that had been underlined by her grandmother. She paused to read verses in the forty-sixth chapter of Psalms.

God is our refuge and strength, a very present help in trouble. Therefore will not we fear, though the earth be removed, and though the mountains be carried into the midst of the sea.

The letter written by her great-grandmother spoke to Karin. She recognized that she was confused and lonely. Maybe she should accept the help her friends offered. She began to weigh her options.

If she went to Indiana, she would sleep on the couch in Mary and Jason's apartment. It would be kind of exciting to be with Mary and hear about her pregnancy. If she went to northern Michigan, she would have a room in Abigail's duplex. Abigail's family was nearby and had been so welcoming at Thanksgiving. Although Karin didn't acknowledge it, the thought crossed her mind that Peter was in northern Michigan.

Karin called Jenny to postpone plans for apartment hunting in Chicago. She explained that she was going to be away for a few weeks.

Jenny was glad to hear from Karin but disappointed by the change in plans.

"Let me know as soon as you get back, and then we can reschedule," Jenny said. "By the way, have you heard from Mrs. Sander recently? Is she going to pursue legal action?"

"Actually, yes. Did I tell you I met with a lawyer?" Karin asked and she went on to describe the meeting. She also told her about Dr. Cutter and the clinic.

"Was that the clinic you and I visited?" Jenny asked.

"Yes. It's like a big nightmare to me."

"That Dr. Cutter sounds like a complicated man. I would stay away from him."

"I'm relieved to be going away for a while," Karin admitted.

Chapter 22

KARIN FLEW TO Green Bay, Wisconsin. She was expecting Abigail to meet her, but Evelyn Larson waved to her instead. When Karin's facial expression registered surprise, Evelyn smiled warmly.

"Both Ben and Abigail have a full schedule today. Ben is needed at the hospital, so Abigail is seeing patients at the office. I'm free and happy to meet you. I like coming down to Green Bay." Evelyn said.

Evelyn made every road trip an adventure. She and Karin did a little shopping in Green Bay and stopped by a used bookstore. Evelyn loved books.

Karin took a couple of minutes to get oriented in the overstocked shop. Books were shelved in stacks that went almost to the ceiling. The aisles between the stacks were narrow, and the air was a bit musty. Karin sneezed, and as her eyes adjusted to the dim lighting, she noticed category labels on the shelves. She found an illustrated copy of *Anne of Green Gables*.

"This was one of my favorite books when I was growing up," Karin said.

Evelyn nodded and then squealed with delight, "Look at this!" She held up a book entitled *Kiitos Amerikan Paketista*. On the cover there was a picture of people in plain 1940s clothing. They were holding up a large package.

"Do you know what the title means?" Karin asked.

"I know just a little Finnish, but along with the picture I am guessing that it says 'Thanks for American Packages.'" Evelyn noted that it was published in Helsinki in 1947. She read a brief note in English expressing thanks to American friends who sent letters and packages to Finland during and after World War II.

Evelyn purchased the book, planning to show it to John Aaltio. He would be able to read it and could offer insight into the correspondence with Finland. Evelyn collected literature and documents that helped her understand the Finnish culture in northern Michigan. Perhaps she would teach a class in the future.

Aliisa wept as she read the letter from her sister in Finland. The words swam before her eyes. Destruction and loss of life. Aliisa's nephew had been killed in the winter war with Russia. He fought bravely in the white wilderness and contributed to the amazing resistance of the Finnish army. But he was injured and succumbed to his wounds.

Finland held off against Russia, but because the little country sided with Germany during the war, Finland lost 10 percent of its land and had to pay war reparations to Russia. People were homeless. Refugees from the territories ceded to Russia poured into the shrinking nation. The Finns made room for them in their homes. The landscape changed, but the people were determined to survive with grace and dignity.

That wasn't the end of it. As the German soldiers retreated from their posts they burned and pillaged northern Finland, killing whole families and destroying towns. An uncle's home had been destroyed. Soldiers who had been allies in the fight against Russia now turned on Finland, scorching the earth.

Aliisa thought about her homeland with great sorrow. Food was scarce and luxury items were nonexistent. Coffee was difficult to obtain. Toys, new clothes, and ribbons were not to be had at Christmas.

The decline of the mining industry put a strain on residents of the copper country; Aliisa was making do with less. She still found ways to help the less fortunate in Finland.

Aliisa's tears flowed as she prayed, "Oh God, how could this happen? Please help my relatives." Aliisa had been in the United States for forty years and had raised her children here. But she still dreamed about her homeland and her family members. She could not bear to think of the devastation.

Aliisa focused her energy on sending aid. Along with other women, she packed boxes of clothes, tins of coffee, and toys for the children. They started their meetings with prayer and sang songs as they worked. A wave of supplies was sent and encouraged their countrymen to carry on.

Chapter 23

A S THEY DROVE to Mine Harbor, Evelyn asked Karin about the investigation of Lori's death. Karin related her interview with the lawyer and the discovery that a doctor she knew was involved with the clinic.

"I'm sorry," Evelyn said. "The whole situation is sad."

Karin was sorting through tangled thoughts. She gazed out at the open highway bordered by snow-trimmed evergreens. Evelyn had always displayed kindness and a willingness to listen. Karin pursued a question that was troubling her. "Was it wrong for Lori to take the abortion pill?"

Evelyn was silent for several minutes, weighing her words. Finally she said, "It is human nature for us to take life and its problems into our own hands. We all do that. I'm sure that Lori thought that she was solving a problem. But she didn't have God's perspective. God designed our bodies, and He calls us to pray and seek His guidance."

"I don't think Lori believed in God. What do you think she should have done?"

"I wonder if she received any counseling at the clinic, or if she was able to get a full range of facts. Did she think that abortion was her only option? Did anyone direct her to support and resources for an unplanned pregnancy? We are all connected to this tragedy." Evelyn was voicing thoughts and questions she had turned over in her mind for days. "We live in a broken world. Abortion can be offered to a woman as an easy answer, but there are consequences. The consequences vary and perhaps don't bother some women.

"I believe that God loves women and knows that we face tough situations, but the Bible is clear; God never wants us to take a life. Lori needed help."

"It isn't fair that she died," Karin said.

"No, it isn't fair. We live in a world marred by sin. We will encounter pain and things we don't comprehend. But if we know God, everything will be made right in heaven."

Karin listened. Evelyn's words and kindness made an impression. She thought her great-grandmother would have liked Evelyn. They seemed to have the same attitude toward God. It occurred to her that Mary had similar perspectives.

They had been driving for a couple of hours when Evelyn pulled up to a little cafe. The building was old and had a large display window showcasing coffee paraphernalia. An orange neon sign was lit up with the words "Coffee & Espresso."

"It's time for a coffee break," Evelyn said.

The old cafe had the scent of polished wood mixed with the aroma of rich coffee. They walked up to the counter and saw a dozen jars of coffee beans. A glass case contained scones and shortbread cookies. Evelyn ordered a Peruvian coffee and a blueberry scone. Karin ordered a Guatemalan coffee and a cinnamon scone. The shop owner measured out the coffee beans and made individual brews for the women.

They sat down at a burnished wooden table to enjoy their treat. Karin was developing the skill of handling her cup with her left hand. The cup tipped a little and a drip slipped down her chin. She dabbed at it with the napkin. Evelyn graciously picked up the conversation.

"Mine Harbor is much quieter than Chicago, but we do have universities nearby. Finnish culture is making a comeback with some fun events. In fact, *Heikkinpäivä* begins this week." Evelyn laughed at Karin's puzzled expression.

"Heikkinpäivä is the Finnish word for St. Henry's Day. St. Henry was a Catholic missionary to Finland. He was martyred on January nineteenth, and he was named a patron saint of Finland. Now St. Henry's Day is a mid-winter celebration, and it's been adopted by the city of Hancock."

"Oh, I see," Karin said. "So what happens?"

"Well, on Friday afternoon Rita Aaltio is going to give a demonstration on making Finnish brown bread, like the bread made in Finland years ago. I am going to give Rita a hand. Perhaps you would like to go with me?"

"Sure," Karin replied. She enjoyed being with Evelyn.

"On Saturday there is a parade," Evelyn continued.

"A parade in the snow?" Karin said in wonder. The snow banks were growing as they drove north. The trees, laden with snow, glistened when the sun made brief appearances through the gathering gray clouds.

"Yes, but I'm going to pass on the parade this year. I will attend the concert at the Lutheran church on Sunday."

"Who marches in a winter parade?" Karin said.

"Students from Finlandia University and Michigan Tech. And there are carts and sleighs pulled by horses or reindeer. A couple of bands. And of course, St. Henry."

Evelyn put down her coffee cup. "We should get back on the road."

They arrived in Mine Harbor in the evening and picked up some pasties for dinner. "Yes! I finally get to try a pasty," Karin said.

Evelyn asked Karin what she meant and Karin explained. "When I went to my grandmother's funeral, the pastor said my grandmother had arranged pasty dinners at the church," Karin said. "I've never had one."

The pasties were warming in the oven when Ben and Abigail arrived home simultaneously. Ben said, "It smells good, and I'm hungry."

Abigail gave Karin a big hug. "I'm so glad you are here," she said.

They sat down to a filling meal of meat, potatoes, rutabagas, carrots, and onions wrapped in a savory crust. After dinner Abigail and Karin went to their duplex where Abigail helped Karin settle into her room. Then Abigail suggested a game of Scrabble.

"Wow, I haven't played Scrabble in years. But sure, why not," Karin said. Abigail set up the game and refreshed Karin on the rules. They played intensely and competitively. Abigail put down the word, *wadi*.

"What's a wadi?" Karin said.

"It's the course of a stream during the rainy season, but it dries out part of the year. It's like a winding ditch. There are wadis in Africa."

Karin put down *queen*, placing the q on a triple letter score. "That's thirty-four points for me!"

"Well, watch this. I am going to use all of my letters," Abigail said. She put down the letters, e-c-l-o-g-u-e.

Karin shook her head. "I challenge you. What does it mean?"

"It refers to pastoral poetry," Abigail said, and she opened the dictionary. She turned the pages and showed Karin the entry.

"I get fifty extra points for using all my letters."

"All right, don't rub it in."

They finished the game and discussed plans for the week. Abigail mentioned that she was teaching a prenatal class at the hospital on the following evening. She invited Karin to sit in.

"Sure, I'd like to come along. On Friday I am going with Evelyn to watch your mom's bread-making demonstration."

"That's great. Dad has roped Mom into participating in Heikkinpäivä. Maybe we can go to the parade on Saturday. Paul is going to be marching with a group from Finlandia University." Abigail said.

"My dad tried to get everyone to participate. Ray had a chance to dress up as a bear but he begged off. Dad will be pleased if we go to the parade."

Thursday evening Karin accompanied Abigail to her prenatal class. Abigail led four couples through relaxation exercises and then gave an overview of labor. Her presentation emphasized that labor and birth is a normal process. She explained the importance of paying attention to signals the body gives. She made a point of telling the men that their support was relevant and important.

The couples asked questions and seemed to openly respect Abigail. Karin enjoyed observing and found that she was gaining new insights. Abigail was interesting, almost entertaining to watch. She had a passion for encouraging young women that lit up her instruction.

On Friday, Evelyn picked up Karin shortly after noon. They drove to Hancock and parked by the Lutheran church.

"Rita's class is in the church basement. They have a kitchen and a community room," Evelyn said.

Rita was busy bringing supplies and ingredients from the kitchen to a large table. She wore a bright marimekko apron and a scarf around her head. Evelyn and Karin sat down as a group of women, a couple of men, and students from a high school class filtered in, finding seats.

Rita began by explaining that she would be making the rye bread that was typical of western Finland. The bread was made several times a year and in large quantity. It was shaped with a hole in the center, and after baking hung on poles above the oven. It dried and was eaten as hard crisp bread.

Rita showed them the preliminary rye sour that she had put together the day before. She had mixed together rye flour, rye cracker crumbs, water, and yeast. She had kept the mixture on top of the oven overnight. Now she added more rye flour and yeast, turned the dough out on a floured board, and kneaded it. Then she put the dough into a greased bowl and covered it with a cloth.

"We have to let it rise for an hour. In the meantime we can have coffee and gingerbread cookies." Such fare was always welcome, and everyone lined up for the afternoon coffee break.

Several women approached Rita. One commented, "You know, my grandmother talked about the brown bread. She said she missed the bread her mother made in Finland."

Another woman asked about cookbooks. "Do you have a Finnish cookbook you recommend?" Rita showed her an illustrated volume, published in Finland.

Karin had never attempted to bake bread. She asked Evelyn, "Do you bake your own bread?"

Evelyn said, "I have a couple of recipes that I make, but I also like to get bread and pastry from Brita's Bakery. I would like to learn how to make the special prune tarts. The Keskitalo's Aunt Lily is an expert. She gave me a recipe. Tomorrow I am going to have her over for a visit, and I'll try making a batch."

"Instead of the parade? That's right, you said you were going to take a pass."

"It's going to be so cold, and I promised Aunt Lily I would have her over. Come by after the parade and warm up."

Rita banged a wooden spoon on the table to get everyone's attention. "It's time to shape the loaves." Everyone turned his attention to Rita. She shaped the dough into three round, flat loaves. Then she pushed a jelly jar into the center of each loaf, cutting a hole in the dough. "I am going to let these loaves rise for half an hour and then I'll bake them at 400 degrees for twenty-five minutes. Now, I happen to have three loaves that I baked yesterday."

She began to slice one. "Come on up and taste the bread. If you want, you can butter it."

Evelyn and Karin stayed until the baking was finished and helped Rita clean up. As a reward they sampled the bread fresh from the oven.

The following morning, Abigail and Karin put on layers of clothing. Abigail found a crimson red scarf and hat for Karin. She chose yellow and blue for herself. "It is mid-winter and we need to brighten the day with color."

They found their place along Hancock's main street where the attending crowd found shelter in doorways. A few people stood by the street curb. It was cold.

The Michigan Tech ROTC led as the honor guard for the parade. Behind them was the Michigan Tech Band. A grade school class marched with a sign that read "*Karhu Kaantaa Kylkea.*" The translation was written beneath: "The Bear Rolls Over." A car pulling a small float followed. The float had a pile of leaves and a very tame, costumed brown bear that appeared to be sleeping. While Abigail and Karin watched, he rolled over to his other side.

"So, what is that about . . . the bear rolls over?" Karin said as she waved to the bear.

"It is a Finnish saying. It means that the winter is half over."

Abigail and Karin watched as *Hankooki Heikki* rode down the street in a sleigh pulled by reindeer. "That is Hancock's St. Henry, the King of the parade." People dressed in traditional Lappish costumes followed.

Karin shivered. "We should join the parade. I feel like I need to walk to keep warm."

When John and Paul Aaltio came by, marching with a group from Finlandia University, Abigail said, "Let's go. We can walk behind them."

The parade came to an end, and Abigail and Karin walked by an open field.

Karin noticed a sign for the wife-carrying event. "What's this?"

"Couples compete in a race. The man has to carry his woman to the finish line . . . Hey! That looks like Peter."

Karin looked. She was sure it was Peter and he was carrying a petite young woman in a fur-trimmed parka. Peter never let on about a girlfriend. Who was she? It had to be a serious relationship if they were in the wife-carrying contest. Karin felt a sharp pang of disappointment.

"Come on," Abigail said. "Let's see who wins."

"No, I'm really cold. I think we should head back to the car. Evelyn invited us to stop by this afternoon," Karin said. She was upset, but she tried to convince herself that she was being irrational. There was nothing between her and Peter.

When Peter approached the wife-carrying contest with his camera, a friend from work called out to him, "I just finished in record time. Bet you can't do better,"

"Drat, I missed my chance to catch you on film," Peter replied, ignoring the challenge.

"Come on, let's see you do the course," Tom persisted.

"I don't have a partner," Peter said.

"Aw, c'mon. We can find you a partner. My sister will go with you, won't you Pam?"

The diminutive Pam grinned. "Sure, I'm game."

"So, I can carry you any way I want," Peter said as he slung Pam over his shoulder.

Pam kicked and screamed, "No, no!"

Peter almost dropped her as he put her down quickly. Pam stood up and put her arms around Peter's neck. "Pick me up now."

Peter put his arms under her legs and carried her close to his chest. He would run the course as a joke. And he would beat his friend's time. He did not see Abigail and Karin pass by.

Peter was at ease with women casually. A close relationship was hard and complicated. He had finally decided to try making contact with Brenda over Facebook. He found her on Facebook, and although he wasn't a friend he was able to send a message. He asked her to call him on his cell phone but had not heard from her.

He had received Karin's Christmas card and note. She had written:

Hey Peter, I was surprised and delighted to receive your card and the pictures. The pictures are amazing. Thank-you!!! We did have a good time, didn't we? Come back sometime for another pad thai dinner. Thanks for driving me home. Karin

When Abigail and Karin arrived at Evelyn's home, they were greeted with the scent of rich pastry, a hint of fruit. Evelyn greeted them with a warm smile, and after they removed their coats, she ushered them into the kitchen. "The best time to sample prune tarts is when they are hot," she said.

Aunt Lily was sitting at the table, with the demeanor of a queen. Ray was serving her coffee and fresh tarts. He looked up sheepishly when Abigail and Karin came in.

"So this is where you've been hanging out," Abigail exclaimed.

"Aunt Lily invited me to help with the tart making," Ray said.

Aunt Lily nodded. "*Raymonsta tulee keittaja.* He's got the knack."

Ray beamed with pleasure. Evelyn commented, "We've had a great time."

Karin and Abigail sat down to enjoy coffee and tarts with Aunt Lily and Evelyn. Karin and Abigail described the day's events.

"Peter was in the wife carrying contest?" Evelyn was surprised. "Who was his partner?"

"Didn't recognize her," Abigail replied.

Anxious to change the subject, Karin asked Aunt Lily about the recipe for the tarts. "These are wonderful! What makes the pastry so tender and flaky?"

"Butter. And the right touch."

"Aunt Lily showed us the technique for layering the butter in the dough," Evelyn explained. The girls were content to visit and then noticed the clock.

"Oh, Mom is expecting us at home," Abigail said.

"And I need to bring Aunt Lily back to Evergreen Senior Care. Take some tarts along with you." Evelyn began preparing a plate of tarts for the young women.

"I'll ride back home with you," Ray said to his sister as he picked up a tart from the plate.

"*Hei sitten.*" Aunt Lily waved good-by.

Saturday night was sauna night at the Aaltio home. After outdoor activities the sauna was soothing. Karin was able to relax physically and emotionally as she rested on the wooden bench, watching flickers of flame in the wood stove. Abigail filled a wooden dipper with water and tossed it on the hot stones. Steam rose from the rocks in a burst of heat. The women were quiet, content with the crackle of fire and the sizzle of steam.

After showering and dressing, Karin and Abigail walked out of the sauna into the cold winter night. It was dark without the glow of city lights. "Look at the stars!" Karin exclaimed. The stars sparkled in the night sky and gave a gentle light. The path to the house was visible among the shadows of trees.

"I think this is my favorite part of sauna nights," Abigail said. "It doesn't feel cold; the air is just refreshing. And the sky is magnificent. There's the big dipper . . . and the north star." She pointed above the house.

After everyone had been to the sauna, they enjoyed cold pop. They sat around the dining room table playing a couple of rounds of Boggle, and then fatigue caught up with them. Abigail and Karin arrived back at the duplex worn out from the full day of activity. They fell asleep as soon as they slipped into bed.

On Sunday morning Abigail and Karin got ready for church. They were going to the same one where Mary and Jason were married. The Keskitalos, the Aaltios, and the Larsons would be there also.

Abigail explained that their full-time pastor was returning after a respite. Five weeks ago his son had lost his battle with cancer, and he had taken time off to grieve the death of his son.

When they were seated in church, Karin noticed more of the surroundings. At the wedding she had been focused on Mary. The wooden pews and beams in the church reflected light from the plain chandeliers. Morning light lit up the colorful stained glass windows.

The organist played and the congregation sang traditional hymns from a hymnbook, followed by choruses that were displayed on a large screen. The minister entered the pulpit and looked directly at the people. He had the congregation's full attention.

He began by reading from John 11:17–43. The verses narrated the death of Lazarus, Jesus meeting with Lazarus's sisters, and Jesus' presence at the tomb. The minister said, "I know firsthand that Jesus sees our pain. He saw the grieving relatives at the tomb of Lazarus, and he wept. He knows what it is like to see death from the human perspective. Death is ugly and it is the last enemy to be overcome.

"Jesus has a dual nature, his humanity and his God-nature. He knows that all our problems are not going to be fixed on earth. He calls us to himself and asks us to look toward the resurrection. The time will come when there will be a new heaven and earth."

Karin listened carefully, and tears slipped down her cheek. She had seen the ugliness of death, and it was a burden on her heart. The words from the Bible were opening a festering wound. When her mother died, she had buried the pain. Lori's death had exposed the unresolved grief.

As the pastor was ending his sermon, Karin slipped out. In the privacy of the restroom she put her head down and cried. After the benediction and closing songs, a couple of women entered. Karin washed her face and avoided making eye contact as she left.

Abigail reached out to touch Karin's arm. "Are you okay?"

Karin waved her hand and motioned that she didn't want to talk. After a quick stop at their duplex, they went over to the Larsons' home for dinner. Evelyn noticed that Karin was withdrawn. She invited her to assist in the kitchen.

"What did you think of the church service?" Evelyn asked.

"The minister's message . . . I never heard someone talk about Jesus like that." Karin's voice broke. She took a deep breath, trying to keep her emotions at bay.

Evelyn put her arm around Karin as the tears streamed down Karin's face.

Karin made a concerted effort to explain her tears. "I never knew that Jesus knows about our pain . . . and cares about us."

"He does know our pain, and he wants to help us," Evelyn said.

"How does he help us?"

"He waits for us to cry out to him," Evelyn said.

"How?"

"In words—you acknowledge him as Lord. Jesus died to pay for the sins of the world. You accept his payment and ask him to help you," Evelyn said.

"That is what I want," Karin said. She was ready to make the choice that Aliisa had once made. Evelyn and Karin prayed together.

During the dinner hour Karin was quiet and at peace. After dinner Ben announced, "There is going to be a concert at church tonight. John said the man playing the kantele is excellent. Let's go." There was enthusiastic agreement.

They settled into pews at the church. An older gentleman with gray hair was sitting on a stool and the kantele rested in his lap. It was a triangular wooden box with fifteen strings, similar to a zither.

Karin was entranced by the lilting music. Each pluck of the string on the instrument, made of polished alder wood, produced a bright and clear note. It almost sounded like a bell. The musician played melodies and occasionally added lyrics.

The program listed both folksongs and hymns. Karin tried to catch the soft and rhythmic sounds of the Finnish words.

Hyvä iltaa nyt kullalleis
Hyvää iltaa nyt linnulleis
Hyväs ja hyväs.

Tantsi tantsi nyt kullalleis
Tantsi tantsi nyt linnuilleis
Hyväs ja hyväs.

When the man began to sing, "*Sinusta, Jesus, ma Laulan,*" some of the older folks joined in. Karin guessed it was a Finnish hymn. She especially enjoyed listening to the kantele while it was accompanied by the piano. The music was soothing and Karin was disappointed when the concert was over.

When they left the church, Peter was standing by the door. "Hey, Karin!" he called out. He always turned up unexpectedly.

Karin was taken aback. She did not expect to see Peter, much less have him accost her.

"What brings you here?" Peter said.

"I broke my arm so I am recuperating among friends. Oh, it looks like Abigail is leaving. Can't miss my ride. I have to go," Karin said.

Peter watched her go. He was puzzled by her attitude. Would he ever understand women?

Peter finally received a call from Brenda, and it startled him.

"Hey, Peter this is Brenda. What a shock to see your message on my computer! What's up?"

"Say, you know, I'm sorry. I was kind of a jerk after you had the abortion."

"It took some time for you to conclude that."

"Yeah, time and my friend Jim. I didn't take responsibility for our relationship. I added to your pain when you were in a difficult place. I'm sorry."

"Thank-you, Peter. It means a lot to hear you say that. I've been to an abortion recovery group, and it has helped me put my life back together. I can truthfully forgive you."

Peter struggled to keep his voice steady, "Thank you, Brenda."

"I'm beginning a fresh start in life."

Peter wondered. Was she hoping to get back together?

Brenda continued, "Things didn't work out for us and it's okay. I want to wish you well."

"How are things going?" Peter said.

"I have a good job, and I'm seeing someone new."

"That's good news. I'm glad you called. Keep in touch," Peter said.

"Probably not. We're both moving on. Take care, Peter," Brenda said.

When Peter put down the phone, he sat down for a moment in wonder. This was a gift. Brenda's forgiveness set him free. That phone call went so well Peter decided to risk another. After getting Abigail's phone number from Jim, he tried to reach Karin. Fortunately Abigail and Karin were together, and Abigail handed the phone to Karin.

"It's Peter," Abigail whispered.

"What does he want?" Karin mouthed. Abigail shrugged.

"Hello," Karin said.

"Hi, Karin. This is Peter. I'd like to see you. I mean, maybe we could go out to dinner?"

Karin was taken off guard. "That wouldn't be fair to your girlfriend," she said.

Now Peter was flustered. Did she know about Brenda? How could she know? Finally he said, "I broke up with her a long time ago."

"But you were in the wife-carrying contest," Karin said.

"What?" Peter said. He thought for a moment and then chuckled. "I was at the race but that wasn't my girlfriend. It was all a joke."

"Sure," Karin said.

"Karin, it was a challenge from my coworker. He wanted me to run the race, so I carried his sister. And I beat his time."

"Oh, I see," Karin said. She felt a little foolish.

"I would like to take you out to dinner," Peter repeated. "How about Thursday?"

"Just a second." Karin put her hand over the phone and asked Abigail, "Do we have anything going on Thursday?" Abigail shook her head.

"Okay, sure." Karin and Peter agreed on 6:30 p.m.

On Thursday afternoon Karin was stressed out trying to decide what to wear. She hadn't asked Peter what restaurant they were going to. Abigail was at the hospital. Karin put on the skirt and blouse she had worn to church and decided against it. Finally she put on a pair of jeans and a blue turtleneck sweater. She fussed with her hair and put on turquoise earrings.

Peter picked up Karin at the duplex and they drove along M-203 to Calumet and then turned on to Sixth Street. They passed the Calumet Theater and looked for a parking spot. The Michigan House was at the corner of Sixth and Oak.

"Oh, it's one of the old buildings," Karin said as she sized up the three-story brick edifice.

"Yeah, this building and the Calumet Theater date back to the time when copper was king."

They entered a room that shone with the warm glow of polished oak. A mural of an alpine scene extended above the length of a bar furnished with stools. Wooden booths and tables filled the remainder of the room. A waiter with dark brown hair pulled back in a ponytail greeted them.

"Welcome. You can choose a seat here or in the adjacent dining room." Karin and Peter followed the waiter to a doorway and peeked in.

"Oh, let's sit in here," Karin said. "Wow, this room is a contrast to the bar. Look at that magnificent fireplace." She was facing a wall of dark stonework that reached to the ceiling. The floor of the room was a mosaic of white and colored porcelain tiles. The walls of the room were light green, the color of birch leaves in early summer. Framed paintings and photographs covered the walls. Each square table had a white tablecloth and a little vase of flowers.

"Such different rooms." Karin looked at the waiter quizzically.

"You came through the bar built by the Bosch Brewing Company in 1905. This room used to be the den, or smoking room, that was open to gentlemen only," the waiter replied as he handed them menus. "I'll be back in a few minutes to take your order."

After carefully perusing the menu, Karin ordered pesto pasta and Peter ordered the Michigan House steak. After their orders were placed, they gazed self-consciously at each other.

Peter asked, "How did you break your arm?"

Karin gave him a simplified version of her last night at work.

"Whew, they work you nurses hard if you can't get a decent dinner break. I'm glad that you're getting some time off."

Their conversation was like a dance as they tried to learn more about each other. Both felt the pull of attraction.

Eventually the topic of Karin's great-grandmother came up.

"Did you know that there is a lot of information about Finnish immigrants on the Internet?" Peter had picked up Finnish immigration details living in the Keweenaw Peninsula and hearing tidbits of information from John Aaltio. John had talked about genealogy and methods of tracing ancestors. Peter soaked up ideas about computer capabilities like a sponge.

"You mentioned that when you drove me to Chicago. But I don't have a computer."

"The Finnish Steamship Company kept detailed records. The passenger lists are available online. You might be able to track your great-grandmother's journey. Sometime I could help you look her up, if you want," Peter said.

"That would be cool," Karin said.

"Well, how about Saturday afternoon? We could go over to the Tech library."

Karin's eyes met Peter's gaze and she blushed. He was so intent; she could feel his interest in her. "I'd like that," she said.

On Saturday Peter gave Karin a tour of the Michigan Tech campus. Because he worked in computer support services, he knew all of the buildings. As they walked passed the Electrical Resources Center, he mentioned the museum housed on the fifth floor.

"Tech began as the Michigan Mining School. The school collected rocks for study and eventually arranged them into displays. It's worth seeing. I'd take you up there, but the museum is only open on weekdays."

"It's a collection of rocks?" Karin said.

"Sounds boring to you?" Peter questioned with a twinkle in his eye. "There are some incredible copper specimens. And there are gemstones and semiprecious stones."

They arrived at the library, and Peter led Karin to a computer. They pulled up two chairs. Peter asked Karin for information about her great-grandmother.

"Her name was Aliisa Ahonen. She married Jan Kaartinen. And I found a receipt from the Finnish Steamship Company dated 1902."

Peter googled Finnish Steamship Company and found a link to emigrant passenger lists. "Okay, spell her name for me."

Peter typed as Karin spelled it out. He hit the search button. Karin squealed with excitement when Aliisa Ahonen's named popped up with additional data. Her birth date was March 24, 1883. Her home parish was Kemijarvi in the province of Oulu. She left Finland on the *Polaris* on April 8, 1902, and traveled to Hull, England. From Hull she traveled by train to Liverpool. She left England on board the *Ultonia* and arrived in Boston, Massachusetts on April 24, 1902.

"Wow!" Karin said.

"The Finnish Steamship Company kept thorough records, and Finnish genealogists have been putting this information online," Peter said.

"Can we look up Jan Kaartinen?"

"Sure," Peter said, and he typed in the name and hit search. No record came up.

"Did you spell it right?" Karin said.

Peter typed Jan's name again as Karin spelled it slowly. Nothing.

"Let's try something else." Peter went back to the Google site and typed in *Polaris*. He found a site with emigrant ships and was able to pull up a picture of the *Polaris*.

"Here's a picture of the boat your great-grandmother was on."

Karin studied the steamship that had the capacity for 265 passengers. She tried to imagine her great-grandmother leaving her home country.

Peter typed in *Ultonia* and pulled up another picture. This was a much bigger ship, first used to bring cattle to America.

"I'm not sure I'd want to travel on that boat," Karin said.

"Anything else that you want to look up?" Peter asked.

"I wonder why Jan's name didn't come up," Karin said.

"He didn't get his passage to the United States through the Finnish Steamship Company. He must have come a different way. Do you know if he worked for a mining company?"

"No, why?"

"The Tech archives have records from the Quincy Mining Company. We could see if his name is in their records."

Peter and Karin searched through an index of the Quincy Mining Company.

They came across an entry listing Jan Kaartinen as a trammer from April to November in 1901. "It looks like he worked at the Quincy Mine for less than a year."

"What's a trammer?" Karin asked.

A librarian overheard Karin's question. "Trammers pushed the heavy carts loaded with ore in the mine tunnels. Not a pleasant job."

"Gosh Peter, I'm amazed at how much we found. I feel a little connection with Keweenaw. I wish I had my own computer," Karin said.

"It's essential if you live in an out-of-the-way place like this. It keeps me connected to the world," Peter said. "Well, after our afternoon of research, can I entice you with a seafood dinner? There is a nice little restaurant in Houghton."

Over the next week, Abigail and Evelyn conspired together to persuade Karin to stay in northern Michigan. Abigail explained that she and Dr. Larson could offer her two days a week because one of the office nurses was moving downstate. In addition, the hospital had openings for the evening shift.

Karin said she might be interested, and Evelyn continued to offer persuasive arguments. "I would like to see you join our community. Abigail and I study the Bible together once a week. You could join us."

Karin was drawn by the rhythm of life that she was beginning to feel. It was soothing to her spirit. She wanted to understand more about faith in God. It would be great to study the Bible with Evelyn. But did she want to move so far from the big cities?

Chapter 24

Henry Ford Hospital is one of the largest and most complete hospitals in the country. Located on West Grand Boulevard, a short distance from the General Motors Building.

—Inscription on a postcard, 1950

ALIISA TOOK THE bus to Detroit. Times had changed, and trains from the copper country to Chicago and Detroit were no longer functioning. Deep shaft mining for copper was in decline, and the towns in northern Michigan were waning. Even the trolleys in Calumet were gone. Detroit and the auto industry was the new hub of activity in Michigan.

Aliisa viewed the buildings and cars in Detroit with amazement. The flow of traffic rushed past her. She had never seen so many cars. The streetlights and signs were bright and baffling. She had never learned to drive a car and had spent the past thirty-five years on a farm. This city was buzzing with activity and dazzled her eyes. Her son-in-law, Arvo, picked her up from the bus station.

"How is Marja?" Aliisa asked.

"She and the baby are fine. They will be coming home from the hospital tomorrow," Arvo said. "According to the doctor, everyone stays in the hospital for at least a week."

Marja had given birth to a daughter seven days ago. She rested in bed and the baby was brought to her four times a day. The nursery nurses took care of the infant and taught classes on baby care and formula preparation. Marja wanted to breastfeed her daughter but her nurse suggested formula. The nurse explained that the baby should take one ounce every four hours.

Arvo and Aliisa drove to Henry Ford Hospital. Aliisa looked at the huge modern building with wide eyes. Arvo said, "This is a grand hospital, one of the largest in the country."

They entered the building, and Arvo led the way to the third floor. They came to the room that Marja shared with another woman. After greeting her daughter, Aliisa asked, "Where is the baby?"

"In the nursery," Marja replied. "We can walk there." She reached for a robe, slipped it on, and led the way. She stopped in front of a large glass window and pointed to one of twenty cribs. "There she is."

Aliisa peered through the window, trying to get a glimpse of the baby's face.

The nursery was clean and brightly lit. The floors and counters were polished. The nurses wore white uniforms and white hats. It was impressive and strange to Aliisa.

They visited for a while and then Arvo and Aliisa went home to prepare for Marja and Anne's homecoming. They shopped for groceries and Aliisa planned the meals.

The next day Arvo went to pick up Marja while Aliisa cleaned house and fixed dinner. Arvo was a veteran of World War II and with the help of the GI bill had been able to secure a mortgage for a snug house with two bedrooms. A bassinette was set up in Marja and Arvo's bedroom; Aliisa would stay in the other.

Despite staying in the hospital for a week, Marja was pale and weak. A forcep delivery, heavy bleeding afterward, and a painful episiotomy had taken a toll. Marja needed more time to heal.

Marja walked slowly to the kitchen and showed her mother the large kettle, glass bottles, and nipples. She showed her the formula powder and explained the process of preparing the formula and filling sterilized bottles. "Could you make up some bottles for the baby?"

"You need all this stuff?" Aliisa said. "Just put the baby to breast."

"At the hospital they told me to give formula."

"I will help you breastfeed," Aliisa said. She thought about her own experiences. She would never have been able to take care of her six children if feeding them was so complicated. The baby started to cry and Marja looked as if she was going to cry also.

"Come and sit down," Aliisa said. Aliisa picked up the baby and looked at her with delight. She smiled at this new granddaughter. "Ah, you are a precious bundle."

She handed the baby to Marja and helped her position the baby at the breast. At first baby Anne sucked and cried. The milk came out of the bottle so much faster.

Baby Anne had to learn to suck persistently at the breast. The first day at home was a trial, but Aliisa kept encouraging Marja.

Aliisa prepared food for her daughter and encouraged her to drink fluids. She remembered the care she had received from the midwife. She enjoyed the chance that she had to cradle and coo at her granddaughter. Her years of mothering had been stressful and exhausting. To be a grandma was a well-earned pleasure.

On the second day home when there was a quiet period, Aliisa asked Marja about Anne's birth. "How did it go for you in the hospital?"

"It was fine."

"Wasn't it a great relief when you heard the baby's first cry?"

Marja looked puzzled. "I don't remember that."

"You don't remember?" Aliisa asked with surprise.

"My memory is very patchy. I don't know if I dreamt it, but I think they took me to the delivery room on a cart. Then my arms and legs were strapped down. They put a mask over my face. I was out for a few minutes."

"How can you give birth when you are out?" Aliisa said.

"It's how they do it in the hospital. I remember some pain, and then it was gone," Marja said. "I was laying on my back in the delivery room, with my legs strapped in stirrups. The doctor said that he needed to use forceps."

Aliisa shook her head in disbelief. She had no concept of forceps. "When you were born, Hanna Jarvela and the midwife, Greta, came to help. Hanna caught you and handed you to me. You were born in the sauna—a quiet warm place in the winter."

"Ma, no one delivers in the sauna these days. We have doctors and hospitals."

Aliisa stayed in Detroit for two weeks. She marveled at the cars, the new shopping center, and the busy sidewalks. She wondered about the lifestyle changes that Marja and Arvo were embracing. She was glad that her daughter was living in a thriving city. She wasn't sure what to think about the hospital. But she felt some things were constant. Babies should be breastfed.

Chapter 25

TOWARD THE END of February, Detroit was drab, the trees bare, and the skies often cloud covered. The gray skies reflected the depressed economy. The auto industry was in a downturn. Would Detroit survive as a vital city? It was entering a new season.

Karin was on the threshold of a new season as well. As she rode in a taxi from the airport to Mrs. Sander's home, she reminded herself that spring was coming. She was looking forward to the change of season and a new beginning. She called Jenny to let her know she had arrived in Detroit. "Do you think that you could pick me up from Mrs. Sander's home in an hour?"

"Sure, Karin. I have one errand and then I'll get you."

Mrs. Sander welcomed Karin with a hug. She looked good with a new hairdo and an attractive blue pantsuit. Her living room was in better order than the last time Karin visited. The floor had been picked up and the coffee table was cleared.

"I'm glad you came today. Tomorrow I'm off to Florida. I have a girlfriend there and we're going to sunbathe and pamper ourselves. What happened to your arm?"

"Oh, I broke it with a crazy fall. It was actually a good thing because I've been off work, and I've been able to travel. I've been spending time with friends in Mine Harbor. But I have to get back to Chicago for an appointment with the doctor on Wednesday."

"Want to sit down? How about a soda? I have Pepsi and Sprite," Mrs. Sander offered.

"Sure, I'll have a Pepsi," Karin said.

Mrs. Sander brought Karin a glass and said, "I have news." She smiled broadly and waited for Karin to ask.

"What is it?"

"I've been offered a settlement from the clinic. I can't tell you how much, but it will make my life easier. Thanks for suggesting that I get legal help."

"So, I guess this means that Lori's case won't go to court," Karin said.

"That's right, I want this to be over. I don't want Lori's name to be smeared," Mrs. Sander said. A few tears slipped down her cheek.

Karin put an arm around Mrs. Sander. "I know. I miss Lori. It's hard for me, but it's even harder for you," Karin said.

Mrs. Sander wiped her eyes. She pointed to her suitcases. "It was hard to make the decision to go to Florida. My friend persuaded me that I need a change of scene and some sunshine."

"She's right," Karin said. It was a balancing act to remember Lori and still move forward. It was taking time for Karin to have the energy to make a change. The decision to move forward felt good.

"Aside from your arm, you look good Karin," Mrs. Sander commented.

Karin told her about the three weeks in northern Michigan and her new friends.

"I'm thinking about moving to Mine Harbor," Karin said.

"Really, what will you do there?"

"I could work at the little hospital. And I would have a group of friends. I've met a woman who is helping me learn about God."

Mrs. Sander said, "I don't want anything to do with God. He didn't save my Lori."

Karin started to explain that God cared about her and her pain, but Mrs. Sander shook her head. "Don't talk to me about God."

Their conversation was winding down when the doorbell rang. Mrs. Sander opened the door and there was Jenny with a big grin. "Hello, Mrs. Sander. I'm looking for a nurse who was injured on the call of duty. Is the brunette here?"

"She's here," Mrs. Sander said as she turned to Karin.

Karin extended her hand to Mrs. Sander and she gripped it tightly for a minute. Karin kissed Mrs. Sander gently on the cheek, "I hope you have a good trip."

Mrs. Sander replied, "I won't forget you, Karin. Take care of yourself."

As they walked to her car, Jenny told Karin with glowing eyes that she was planning to accept a position at a university hospital in Chicago. "I'll be working in the oncology unit and learning some of the new treatment plans for cancer patients. The salary is great. It's in the opposite direction from Northland, but it should be a similar commute," Jenny said. Her words came out in an excited stream.

The women got into the car and Jenny started the engine. As Jenny guided the car down the street, she glanced at Karin, "Aren't you pleased?"

Karin bit her lip; she needed to be honest with Jenny. She realized that she had come to her decision. Her stomach churned as she gathered courage to speak. She had to tell Jenny about her change in plans. "I'm sorry, Jenny. I'm not going to stay in Chicago. I'm planning to go to northern Michigan for at least the summer," she explained.

Jenny's face fell. "You have to be kidding. You would give up Chicago to go to the backwoods of Michigan? You're going to pull out on me?"

"I know it seems crazy, but I have given it a lot of thought. It's something I need to do." Karin tried to keep eye contact with Jenny.

"I'm hoping you might know another nurse that wants to relocate to Chicago," Karin said.

"No. I wanted to room with you."

"Oh, gosh Jenny. It's just that things are changing in my life. When I was in northern Michigan I was able to sort things out." Karin felt terrible letting her friend down and almost wavered in her decision.

"It's that guy, Peter, isn't it?" Jenny said.

"No, it's not Peter."

"Right." There was disbelief on Jenny's face.

"I mean not just Peter. It's other things. It's the community there. Abigail's family, Dr. Larson and Evelyn have been really good to me. Their support means a lot. Evelyn is very wise, and she has offered to study the Bible with me."

"So you're going to become religious." Jenny turned away. "Our plans didn't mean anything to you."

"Jenny, I want to stay friends—I just need to do this. If you want to come out to my apartment sometime in the next few weeks, you can come and stay. You can bring a friend with you," Karin offered. "My lease is up at the end of April."

Karin wanted Jenny to understand, but Jenny was greatly disappointed. Her carefully laid plan was falling apart. The remainder of their time together was strained. When it was time for Karin to catch the train, they were both relieved.

Karin had an inner confidence that she was making the right decision, but it was hard to respond to Jenny. Karin hoped that somehow she could keep a close friendship with Jenny.

Chapter 26

HE TRAIN CLATTERED along the tracks, and Karin rested in her seat, thinking about the things Evelyn said. As the train approached Kalamazoo she took out her cell phone and called Abigail. She told Abigail she had made up her mind. She was planning to come to Mine Harbor. "Is the office position still open?"

"Yes!" Abigail said. "It's just a couple of days a week, but I am sure that you could also get a part-time position at the hospital. And you can share the duplex with me—that is if you want to."

"Of course I want to!" Karin said. It would be interesting to live with this confident and resolute midwife. They talked and planned Karin's move to Mine Harbor.

Karin's cast came off when she saw the doctor. He gave the okay for her to return to work at Northland the following week. Karin went but at the same time brought a letter of resignation.

When she gave it to the nurse-manager, the manager asked her to sit down. "Does this have anything to do with Dr. Cutter?"

Karin sat back in her chair, speechless. She had never mentioned Dr. Cutter's involvement with the clinic. Or was it about the times she met Dylan for a drink? Did everyone know she had been out with him?

The manager continued. "Dr. Cutter complained to me about your performance. He said that you didn't give enough personal attention to his patients."

The heat rose in Karin's face. She sputtered. The accusation was ludicrous.

The manager said, "Don't get upset. I talked to your coworkers, and I know that you do a good job. He was irrationally upset. I told him that I would avoid having you take care of his patients, but I am doing that for your sake. Is your decision to leave related to Dr. Cutter? I really don't want to lose you. You are a good nurse."

Karin sighed. How to explain this? "There are many other factors. I am moving to a community where I have friends. It's a positive move, and I am looking forward to a change."

"All right, Karin. But if you ever want to come back, we'd be glad to have you."

Her coworkers were curious about her decision. "How big is this town that you are going to?" they asked.

"It's pretty rural," Karin said. Every now and then she had a tremor of doubt but didn't show it. At the hospital she kept her attention on her work, but as soon as her shift was over, she turned her focus to packing up her apartment.

When she was leaving the hospital one day, Dr. Cutter walked by her and then stopped. He glanced around and seeing that they were alone said, "Look, your friend's mother received a settlement. I hope you can let it go. I'd appreciate it if you kept quiet about the whole thing." He pushed his glasses up on his nose.

"I'm not going to talk about your involvement with the clinic. I am going to do my best to give women complete information. You know, you talk about giving women what they want. You run a successful business. But shouldn't you be protecting women's health?"

Dr. Cutter put his hand up in a motion to stop Karin's questions. "I don't have time for this." He walked away.

Karin marched off to her car, emotions frazzled. She turned her thoughts to moving. She didn't want to take all of her belongings with her. She had given her kitchen table and chairs to a coworker. She needed to arrange a pick-up from the Salvation Army for her worn sofa and Lori's bedroom furniture.

Jenny called her on the weekend. She was in the midst of new plans. "Have you heard about the demand for travel nurses?" she asked Karin. "I'm looking into it. I could take three- or six-month assignments in hospitals around the country. It would give me the opportunity to work in Chicago and other cities. And I will have more flexibility in planning time off. You left me high and dry, but at least I have an alternative."

"I hope you will visit me," Karin said. "Everyone says Mine Harbor is beautiful in the summer." She planned to keep in touch with the pert redhead.

As all of the details began to fall into place, Karin experienced peace with her decision. Her dad offered to get a U-haul and help her move the remainder of her things. He was having a hard time getting his mind around Karin's decision to leave Chicago and move to Michigan's Upper Peninsula. But he loved his daughter and was willing to support her. He was also a little bit curious about the community she was going to.

They drove a U-haul, towing Karin's car behind. When they came to the two-lane highway in northern Michigan, Mr. Lindale remembered the trip he had made with his wife when Karin was a baby.

She had been just a couple of months old. He had been the proud father. He had taken Lamaze classes with Anne and had stayed with her throughout her labor.

He had held Anne's hands and at times did the slow breathing with her. He remembered the moment Anne had said, "Don't touch me!" The nurse had reassured him that he was doing fine. Anne was going through transition.

When Karin was born, he and Anne had been jubilant. The memories rolled over Brent Lindale. Anne, Brent, and baby Karin had shared a cottage on Portage Lake with Marja and Arvo. They swam in

Portage Lake. Anne and Brent took a rowboat out on the water while Marja watched Karin. These were tender and painful memories.

When Mr. Lindale and Karin stopped for lunch, he said, "Tell me about your new friends."

Karin mentioned the Aaltios. "They have a fabulous sauna. Every Saturday night is sauna night." Brent nodded. He remembered Anne talking about saunas.

She described Abigail, but she spent the most time talking about Evelyn.

"She used to be a literature teacher at a community college and is interested in everything. She is involved in events around Houghton and Hancock and knows what's happening. But she also knows the Bible and knows God."

"What do you mean?" Mr. Lindale said. He didn't want Karin to become a religious fanatic.

"I have been struggling with Lori's death. I don't know why she had to die. Evelyn explained that our world is messed up by sin. Jesus understands this. He understands our pain and wants to help us. We need to ask for forgiveness and guidance." Karin said.

Mr. Lindale looked away. Karin's words cut to his heart. Maybe she was right. He finished his coffee and glanced toward Karin.

"Are you done?" he asked.

Karin nodded.

"Okay, let's go. We still have a long drive ahead of us."

Despite the late hour, Abigail was waiting for their arrival and walked out to the U-haul to help Karin and her father with their luggage. "We can unpack the rest of your stuff tomorrow morning. My brother Paul is coming to help."

"I have the pullout couch for you, Karin." Abigail turned to Mr. Lindale and said, "Ben and Evelyn have offered you their guest room."

They put Karin's suitcase down in the duplex and walked next door. Abigail rang the doorbell and Evelyn came to greet them. She gave Karin a hug and extended her hand to Brent Lindale. "I'm very happy to meet you. You have a lovely daughter."

She explained that she had a pot of tea ready and led them into the kitchen. "Ben is at the hospital tonight, but we've planned a celebration meal for tomorrow. You'll have a chance to meet him then."

They talked briefly about the drive from Chicago and Brent's business trips as they sipped tea. Then Evelyn showed Brent the guest room, and the girls headed back to the duplex.

The following day Paul and Abigail helped Karin and her dad move all of Karin's boxes and furnishings into the duplex. Abigail and Karin directed the men in moving and placing the few pieces of furniture that Karin had brought along.

In the evening Paul, Jim, Lynne and Abigail joined Karin and her father at the Larsons' home. Evelyn had prepared a feast: trout, potatoes au gratin, broccoli, a carrot salad, and fresh rolls. Mr. Lindale glanced around the table as they sat down to dinner. It was a pleasant group of people. He was also touched by the generous hospitality of Ben and Evelyn. Maybe the move to Mine Harbor was a good thing for Karin.

Karin was enjoying the meal but trying to overcome her disappointment. Peter had not come by the duplex, and he wasn't at the dinner. She listened with a distracted ear to the table conversation. Comments centered on upcoming events and the anticipation of summer.

"Copper Harbor is at the tip of the peninsula, and they host an art fair," Lynne said. "We'll have to show you our favorite picnic spot along the way."

When the doorbell rang, Ben jumped up to get it. He brought Peter with him to the dining room, and asked Paul to shift his chair and make room. Mr. Lindale noticed his daughter's face light up.

"I'm sorry I'm late for your party, Karin," Peter said.

"Well, tell her what you were doing, young man," Ben demanded.

"Dr. Larson had an extra laptop computer at his office. He's giving it to you for personal use. I wanted to get it all ready. After dinner I can show it to you," Peter said.

Karin's face shone with joy. She looked around the table at her new circle of friends. She felt blessed. "Thank-you Dr. Larson and Peter." Her gaze lingered on Peter and he blushed with pleasure.

"We want you to stay," Evelyn said. "Anyone for blueberry pie and coffee?"

Endnotes

Chapter 1

Copper Country Evening News, Engel, Dave and Gerry Mantel, *Calumet, Copper Country Metropolis*, 23.

Chapter 7

Copper Country Evening News, Engel and Mantel, *Calumet, Copper Country Metropolis*, 25.

Chapter 9

Calumet News, Engel and Mantel, *Calumet, Copper Country Metropolis*, 126.

Chapter 11

Calumet News, Engel and Mantel, *Calumet, Copper Country Metropolis*, 200.

Chapter 12

1. *"She stepped, tripped along"*; Bosley, Keith, Michael Branch and Matti Kuusi, eds. *Finnish Folk Poetry Epic*, 288-9.

2. *The actual text of the oath*; Eliot, Charles W. ed., *The Harvard Classics, 3.*
3. *I will follow that method*; http://physiciansforlife.org.
4. *Ben had looked at research studies*; Kahlenborn, Chris, *Breast Cancer*, 133-4.

Chapter 13
Kolehmainen, John. *The Finns in America*, 126-7.

Chapter 15
Rajanen, Aini, *Of Finnish Ways*, 98.

Chapter 23
1. "Heikkinpäivä"; http://pasty.com.
2. "Hyvä iltaa ny kullaleis . . "; http://kantelemusic.com.

Bibliography

Bosley, Keith, Michael Branch, and Matti Kuusi. *Finnish Folk Poetry Epic*. Helsinki: Finnish Literature Society,1977.

Dick-Read, Grantly M.D. *Childbirth Without Fear*. New York: Harper Paperbacks, 1984.

Eliot, Charles W., ed. *The Harvard Classics, Volume 38*. New York: P.F. Collier & Son, 1910.

Engel, Dave and Gerry Mantel. *Calumet, Copper Country Metropolis*. Rudolf, Wisconsin: River City Memoirs, 2002.

Foote, William M.D., and Harry Oxorn M.D. *Human Labor and Birth*. New York: Appleton-Century-Crofts, 1975.

Kahlenborn, Chris M.D. *Breast Cancer: It's link to Abortion and the Birth Control Pill*. Dayton, Ohio: One More Soul, 2000.

Kolehmainen, John. *The Finns in America*. Hancock, Michigan: Finnish Lutheran Book Concern, 1947.

Larson, Amanda Wiljanen. *Finnish Heritage in America*. Marquette, Michigan: The Delta Kappa Gamma Society, 1976.

Leney, Terttu. *Teach Yourself Finnish*. Chicago: NTC Publishing Group, 1975.

Meier, Gene. *Askel Means Step*. Hancock, Michigan: Book Concern Printers, 1983.

Monette, Clarence. *Hancock Remembered: vol. 1*. Calumet, Michigan: Greenlee Printing Co., 1982.

Monette, Clarence. *Houghton County's Streetcars and Electric Park*. Calumet, Michigan: Greenlee Printing Co., 2001.

Monette, Clarence. *Laurium Michigan's Early Days*. Calumet, Michigan: Greenlee Printing Co., 1986.

Murdoch, Angus. *Boom Copper*. Hancock, Michigan: The Book Concern Printers, 1966.

Rajanen, Aini. *Of Finnish Ways*. New York: Barnes & Noble Books, 1984.

Rantamaki, John E., translated by Helmar Peterson. *A Morsel of Finland into a Wild Wilderness; A History of Otter Lake*, 1995.

Rislakki, Eero. *Kiitos Amerikanpaketista*. Helsinki: Mantere. 1947.

Schnieder, Lisa. Ladies Society's Inner Workings Revealed. *Finnish American Reporter*. October 2007.

URLs

"Free Stuff; Lyrics to Traditional Finnish Folk Songs";
http://kantelemusic.com

"Restatement of Hippocratic Oath (A.D. 1995)";
http://physiciansforlife.org/content/view/28/29

"Heikkinpäivä"; http://pasty.com

PW

To order additional copies of this book call:
1-877-421-READ (7323)
or please visit our Web site at
www.pleasantwordbooks.com

If you enjoyed this quality custom-published book,
drop by our Web site for more books and information.

www.winepressgroup.com

"Your partner in custom publishing."

LaVergne, TN USA
24 June 2010
187317LV00003B/1/P